ERIK HARALDSSON

ERIK HARALDSSON

YELLOW HAIR
BOOK ONE

RON BRIGGS

WOLFPACK
PUBLISHING
— EST 2013 —

Erik Haraldsson
Paperback Edition
Copyright © 2024 (As Revised) Ron Briggs

Wolfpack Publishing
1707 E. Diana Street
Tampa, Florida 33609

wolfpackpublishing.com

Paperback ISBN 978-1-63977-648-1
eBook ISBN 978-1-63977-647-4

FOREWORD

FOREWORD

This is a work of fiction. The characters, events, and places are contrived by the author. An honest attempt has been made to describe real cultures and interactions as they may have taken place early in the eleventh century AD.

The story begins with Erik Haraldsson on a voyage to prove his manhood by killing a polar bear on the arctic ice near Greenland. Erik turned sixteen years old on the voyage and is anxious to attain glory. His experiences on the voyage change his mindset from desiring glory to making changes in Norse attitudes.

The cultures depicted as interacting in this story are the Norwegian Norse, Greenlandic Norse, Icelandic Norse, and Dorset culture.

This first book of the saga deals with a young

Norseman who is influenced by his experiences while on a voyage to Greenland in his late teen years. He passes on his lessons to his son, who will be a major focus of the rest of the series. The characters and places described are fictional. A few historical figures are mentioned, but no interactions with fictional characters occur in the story.

ERIK HARALDSSON

CHAPTER 1
ERIK HARALDSSON

E rik sat quietly listening to the rhythmic slapping of the waves against the strakes of the ship while his eyes strained for light to see the rugged coastline. His caribou coat and leggings, wolfskin hat and mittens, and wool-lined leather boots kept the cold at bay for the most part.

The sounds of ropes stretching and straining through the pulleys, against the tie blocks, and the ship's planks creaking as the big knorr rolled gently through the low swells was a mere whisper compared to the sounds created in the wild, open waters after they left Iceland. *We must be well into ice bear country by now*, he thought. *But, for the love of all that is holy, all I can make out are the snow-covered hills to the east. That could be ice along the shore, I just can't be sure. The shoreline appears to be shrouded in drifting fog.* The unusually still night sky cast almost no light on the land.

They were three days and nights north out of the Western Settlements of Greenland and Erik was ready for some action. The first two nights Haakon steered the ship into one of the many fjords the coast offered as safe harbors. But last night brought a soft, steady southern breeze, and as they traveled north, the fjords were becoming clogged with more ice all the time. With the help of the stars and a dim half-moon, Haakon was able to keep the ship on a safe course. That moon had now set, and the only light was afforded by the plentiful stars, but a thin layer of high clouds drifting overhead had muted the light from that source. In addition, curtains of faint green and purple undulated across the sky. The Lights were faded by the thin clouds, but still reflected dimly on the ice and snow of the hills to the east and faintly on the dark waters of the Greenland Sea.

Erik had been rather bored with the Greenland coast for the most part. Fjords and snow-covered hills were all there was to see. Even the more jagged fjords did not hold the powerful beauty of Norway's. *And these hills are nothing compared to the mountains of the homeland. Yet, there is a kind of stark beauty here that keeps me staring at it,* Erik mused

2

inwardly. The total lack of life was something new to him. He could not even see an animal track blemishing the blanket of new snow over the land. As they moved up the coast, the hills became gentler, and the low brush all but disappeared from the valleys. Also, the snow laid deeper on the land—the longer days had not yet affected this region like they had around Brattahlid and the Western Settlements. The sun's rays were just not strong enough yet to break the coldness this far north.

The day before, they had sailed by two small, rounded snow-covered hills that drooped down to the sea with but a tiny, narrow bay between. Cousin Olaf had pointed to the formation and said, "Erik, imagine them as the breasts of a woman. Picture them as the perfect woman, her breasts looking like those round hills covered with soft, white skin, like the cream that rises to the top of fresh milk early on a cold morning. That image came to me when we sailed by this very spot two years past, when on Haakon's last voyage to Greenland. Now, imagine burying your face between those breasts!" Olaf always had a way of laughing at the world.

The long night gave Erik much time to think. His thoughts wandered from the conflict he had with his father, to dreams of killing an ice bear, to imagining all sorts of adventures on this trip. He even thought about what he would do if he encountered a Skræling.

All he'd ever heard about them was that they were dirty, clothed in animal skins, and bloodthirsty thieves. They were impossible to trade with, for they could not understand the spoken word, and their own tongue consisted of strange grunts and animal sounds. They were probably more animal than human. From what he knew, there was no word of them in Christianity, and he could not remember a reference to them in the old pagan stories. *They must be lower than thralls, if they are human at all*, he presumed. He had heard that they would not engage in any kind of trade talk for very long before they began fighting.

The stories told Erik the Skræling weapons were crude but deadly. *It must be true that they use some sort of poison on their stone arrow points because I know of two people who had been wounded and died a short time later. The descriptions of their deaths were ghastly.*

His own grandfather reportedly laid in a bed for three days in Brattahlid after they brought him back from Vinland, moaning the strangest things and screaming out in pain before drowning in pus from the arrow in his chest. His father said he

4

could remember the terrible stench that arose from the dying man's weakening body.

And yet, Haakon said they would seek a Skræling village he had heard was friendly, and willing to trade some worthless wool strips for fine walrus ivory. *In any case, if I encounter a Skræling, I will kill the animal like a cockroach, just for grandfather,* he promised himself.

Occasionally a block of ice would float out of the darkness toward them, taking Erik away from his thoughts. He would yell back to Haakon the size and course of the ice block, and Haakon would take appropriate action. Some blocks were so small that Haakon would allow the sturdy ship to push them aside. Others would require changing course to avoid damage. Twice since they left the Western Settlements he had seen large icebergs far to the west. The huge blocks of ice looked like floating mountains. *A whole camp of Norse warriors could set up on one and drift to some foreign land to conquer it,* he imagined.

Curse the darkness of this land! Erik's eyes pressed into the darkness that lay to the front of the ship. *Is it fog or just darkness that stares at me?* He could not tell.

Faintly, out of the darkness he began to see a shape. It was a large iceberg straight ahead on their course. A frantic cry burst from his lips,

"Haakon! Big iceberg, straight ahead! It appears to be drifting south and to our port side."

Haakon's voice thundered in the darkness, "Up, men! Oars into ports! Steerboard oars, back stroke, full power! Port oars, full ahead! Make haste, men! It is no time to dally!" Men sprang from their resting places and went to work without hesitation. Erik marveled at Haakon's absolute authority over these men, at least while on the ship. Yet, no one ever spoke badly of him.

As they drew near the iceberg, Haakon ordered, "Port side, ship oars!" The ship slid along the edge of the ice for several heartbeats that seemed like hours, barely bumping the massive chunk of ice once or twice. Erik noticed a sudden chill in the air next to the huge ice block. The few torches that had been lit made its milky blue-green color mesmerizing. Until the iceberg was right upon them, the only color Erik saw was white, but right there in front of his eyes, he was able to see the true milky blue-green color. He wished for bright sunlight to study the ice better. As it was, the closeness was only there for a fleeting moment as their course took them northeast while the berg was drifting south and west. When they passed clear of it, all the men gave out a rowdy cheer, and the ship's direction was corrected back to due north.

Erik was still trembling, partly from the cold and partly from the fright. The others settled back into their sleeping blankets. He had no desire to get that close to a big iceberg again. But as the terror left him, he began to feel a sense of accomplishment—something he had precious little of in his life. Now, his warning had been what saved the ship from disaster! "A fair omen for what lies ahead," he whispered.

After a while, with no more hazardous chunks of ice spotted, only Haakon and three others were awake. Haakon manned the steerboard in his typical masterful manner, while the others trimmed the sail at his command. Even in this arctic darkness, Haakon was able to guide the ship north with the light breeze and only the stars to guide him. Only the hills of the jagged shoreline were barely discernible in the darkness. The pale arctic stars gave little light to the land, and the moon had long since disappeared from the night sky. Haakon, however, had plied these waters a few times before and knew where he wanted to go.

Erik had begged to be lookout at the front of the ship to scan for icebergs and chunks of the ice floes that, by now, were breaking up and drifting south toward the open ocean. He looked up at the sky. The stars were drifting in and out of view above the thin veil of clouds. He could name some of the stars, even a few constellations, but for the most part, the night sky was just a giant puzzle. The stars just seemed to be randomly scattered with little rhyme or reason. To make matters worse, they kept moving all night and changed with the seasons. He did not understand how a man like Haakon could get so skilled at reading stars. *Maybe someday I will learn.*

Olaf is lucky to have a father like Haakon who can teach him so much about the world, Erik thought. His own father, Jarl Harald Rolfcarlsson, riveted with a fear of the sea since he was a young man, seldom left Ulfrstadt and never went on a ship that would be going beyond the sight of land. When Harald witnessed his own father's death, he was already nineteen winters old, but the experience changed his life. He had vowed to his wife and to his mother that he would never leave Norway again.

Harald had stayed on the ship when the others went to try to trade with Skræling in Vinland, preferring to learn more about the ship's construction, rather than try to communicate with a bunch of slow-witted, non-human creatures. Watching his father's horrible death that way left quite a mark, for he kept his word all the years since.

True, Father was Jarl of Ulfrland and had become a wealthy stockman and shipbuilder, and was well respected by all who knew him, but Erik wanted adventure. He needed the friendship and rowdiness of a ship full of lusty Norsemen. He could settle down in later years and run his father's farm. Erik had to fight to drive off the thoughts of the arguments he and his father had before leaving on this adventure.

We should pass by the island with the old village on it by daylight. Olaf says they called it a village for lack of a better word. It was just a few shallow dugout rings lined with rocks in the gravel. Olaf had shared all he knew of the place but showed little interest. The village must have belonged to some Skræling of long ago. Olaf had said nothing of value was to be found there, Erik thought about their conversation and was fascinated by the stories and wanted to see the dugout houses for himself. *Olaf had been there but did not mention anything about their roofs or doorways or fireplaces or anything that would make them livable. He had only said they weren't worth looking at. Olaf had found a small ice bear carved from a whale tooth, but in the days that followed, he had lost it somewhere. "It wasn't worth much, anyway,"* Olaf had guessed. Erik recalled every word Olaf had said about the place.

How could anyone live through the winters this far north? Erik pondered. He had heard that Midwinter's Night lasted for months up here. Surely that could not be true. But even at Thorkell's farm in

9

the Western Settlements, the winter nights were longer than in Ulfrstadt, where the winter sun did not climb far into the sky before it started going down. Erik was not interested in spending another winter in Greenland, let alone this far north. *Those Skræling must have lived there during a warmer time, and when the winters got colder, they all died*, he reckoned.

Gradually a grayness spread across the sky and descended on the land and sea. The sky above changed slowly from starlit blackness to gray to deep purple to faint blue. A pale orange backlit the snow and ice-covered hills to the east. Farther north, Erik could see the tops of the high hills of the island. The western and southern coastlines were clear, but the fjord in which the island lay appeared to be frozen solid through the drifting fog. He could see more icebergs and chunks of ice frozen in the wide fjord. A wide, open channel came into view, in which floated various-sized chunks of ice and a couple of small icebergs. He guessed that the big iceberg they had nearly collided with must have flowed out of that chan-nel. It would have been a close fit.

Occasionally following a low rumble, a wave would ripple down the channel pushing ice along out into the sea. He had not known what caused the waves or the sound but learned from a seaman experienced in those waters that large chunks of ice breaking off a glacier and falling into the fjord caused the waves and the sound.

As they neared the island, he noticed a bird had taken to the air from near the top of a high hill. As it got closer, he could see that it was silvery white. It climbed in the sky, and he could tell from the shape it was a falcon. It flew toward the ship, apparently thinking the ship's banner was prey. When the raptor realized its mistake, it flared and flew back toward the hills, screeching its displeasure at the ship.

"It was one of those white gyrfalcons!" he exclaimed to no one. He had seen one that was trained for hunting, but never a wild one. He marveled at how beautiful it was, its flight powerful and unrestrained.

The others began to stir in their thick wool and skin blankets and caribou skin overcoats. Erik could hear some grumbling and typical early morning shipboard chatter. The sound of urine hitting the sea became more frequent as the men woke up and tended to their personal needs. Once or twice, he heard someone break wind followed by jeering from those close by. He hoped Olaf would come up front to keep him company. Erik was not about to give up his vantage now that he could see what lay ahead. He wondered where on that piece of land the old "village" was located. As far as he could tell, the snow and ice lay too deep to find anything at the ground level. *Looks like another disappointment,* he thought. Of course, Olaf had visited the place in late summer when the site was clear of snow and ice.

Expecting to see open sea as the ship slid past the western side of the island, they were instead surprised to see a flat expanse of sea ice stretching to the west. Large blocks of ice were heaved up in many places, and a few narrow bodies of open water could be seen.

CHAPTER 2
THE BEAR

Haakon followed the edge of the sea ice to the west after they skirted around the big island on the coast of Greenland. He expected to find the Skræling village he sought after four days sailing westward along the ice to the southern shore of Helluland. It was now morning on the second day along that course.

As the ship slid along about a couple hundred paces off the edge of the ice, Erik kept his eyes peeled, looking for bears. He wanted to kill one before they reached the Skræling village. With the fog and clouds, it was difficult to tell if he was seeing land to the west or not.

Out on the ice to the north, near an ice block, was a seal, the first he had seen that day. It saw the ship and slipped into a hole in the ice. He had been told that they have breathing holes. They haul out next to them to rest, sun themselves, and in season, give birth to their pups. The season for pups was upon them. This one just slipped into the hole leaving only the brown stains of its feces.

Then he noticed a movement farther out on the ice. It was a bear! *It is limping! And looks very big! Oh, I want him!* "Look, Olaf—bear! We must go get him! Haakon, bear, out on the ice!" Olaf had just come over to join Erik at his lookout. The bear was now about 400 paces away. He saw the ship and stood up on his hind legs and sniffed at the air like he was trying to assess something he had never seen before. He turned and moved back toward the west, away from the ship.

Haakon calmly called Lathan to him. Together they talked quietly for a short time, Lathan nodding most of the time. Finally, Haakon stated, "Lathan, Erik, and Keir will take Vigi, Gilfr, and Floki and run that bear down. A crew will follow tomorrow morning to haul the bear skin and meat back to the ship. Now get the hunting party onto the ice pack so they can get after that bear."

———

It was past midday by the time Lathan's hunting party was on the ice pack and ready to start after the bear. First, they would have to search until they found his tracks. *It should not be too hard because of the way he was limping. I could tell he was injured, and when he stood up, there was blood on his front foot. I wonder how that happened. Could a seal bite him? Maybe another bear.* Lathan was thinking about the best way to wear the bear down.

Erik was beaming with excitement as they neared the area where they last saw the bear.

When they cut the track, Lathan quickly determined, "Something has split the bear's smallest toe from the others on his right front paw. Maybe a sharp rock, perhaps sharp ice? Hard to imagine. Surely no hunters around here—too far from land. It was still bleeding when he made these tracks but is not a real threat to the animal. It will heal in time and probably not bother him. But, for now, he is easy to track. I want to have him killed before sundown. It looks as though a storm is brewing in the southwest and may come this way. A lot of new snow will make our job all the harder."

They followed the tracks, moving southwesterly now, into the sun which was still above the gathering clouds. As they moved along, they gradually separated slightly. Erik did not want the bear diverting off to the north and to miss the opportunity. Moving along, he did not realize he was drifting further from Lathan and Keir. Making things more confusing was the fact that the ice was more and more broken and heaved into irregular blocks.

Suddenly, he felt a shudder under his feet, then a loud rumbling sound followed by a long, sharp *CRACK*. He lost his balance and fell down with the violent shaking under him. Without warning, a body of water opened between him and the others. It was too wide for him to jump, and it extended far behind and in front of him. *What do I do?* he asked himself. After looking around, he decided he might be able to get past the gap before the others got to the bear. He hurried on his way as close to the edge of the lead as he dared.

Eventually he came to the end of the lead and moved back to the south. Now he was all alone, and thickening clouds obscured the sun, which had already begun its descent toward setting. It was becoming more difficult to tell which way was west. He looked in all directions and saw nothing but white sky, white snow, and white chunks of ice.

Erik stopped and listened while catching his breath. The only sounds were the pounding of his heart in his ears, the eerie whistling and moaning of the wind as it blew through and around the heaved blocks of ice and snowdrifts, and the slight tinkling sound of loose snow blowing across the landscape. Finally, he caught a glimpse of figures moving far ahead of him between ice blocks. He hurried toward the sighting as fast as he could.

Soon, he thought he might have heard dogs barking excitedly. As he closed, he definitely heard a dog yelp, then more frantic barking. Another yelp. *This bear must be a fighter.* He tried to move even faster. *Was that water splashing?* Another gurgled yelp. He came around a block of ice to see two dogs dead and bloodied on the edge of a small body of water. The bear, now out of the water, was just catching Keir. The young man was batted to the ground by a swift swat, then pounced on. The bear finished him off with a crushing bite to the back of his skull. The boy's scream was cut short, and his body fell limp.

Now the bear turned his attention to Lathan who was shouting and approaching around the water's edge with his spear ready for a lunge. The bear ran right at him and swatted the spear away like it was a toy. Lathan was able to pivot and take a step, but the bear caught him by the foot and pulled it up to its mouth. Lathan cried out in agony as the bear clamped down on his lower leg.

Without thinking, Erik charged the bear with every bit of energy he could muster. Just as he approached from behind, the bear, with Lathan's leg clenched in his teeth, started to shake the life from its victim. As the bear's body swung, Erik's spear, by luck of chance, drove into the bear's right side just below the ribs and plowed through its vital organs, including stomach, liver, a lung, and finally heart, before lodging between two vertebrae. The bear's reflex action was to pivot its body toward the wound. That action ripped the spear from Erik's hands and snapped the shaft off inside the bear's body. The move also rammed the spear point between the vertebrae and severed the spinal cord, instantly paralyzing the big animal. Erik was only aware that the spear was no longer in his hands, and he turned to run. His feet tangled, and he fell on his face in the snow. Knowing what was coming next, he tried to cover the back of his head. All he heard was a big "whump" as the bear collapsed at his feet.

Erik looked back to see the bear's face. Gone was the sleek, fierce warrior. Instead, Erik looked at what appeared to be a tired old man. The bear's face was round rather than arrow-shaped. The nose was a glob of black scar tissue with a fresh gash, probably from one of Haakon's dogs. The ears were tattered and scarred, several other old scars marked the face, neck, and shoulders. Pink, bloody bubbles issued from the predator's misshapen nose, while bright red streaked with darker red blood oozed from its mouth. The eyes were bloodshot and fading. Black blood flowed from the wound where the spear entered. The chest barely moved with irregular labored breathing. The giant animal's legs stiffened slightly, then went limp.

Erik dropped to his knees and began to weep. His body trembled uncontrollably, and he felt his heart racing, each beat pounding in his ears. *The bear is dead, but at what cost? The dogs, Keir, Lathan...*

Erik heard a moan from the other side of the bear. *Lathan, he lives!* He rushed to find Lathan shivering in shock. *His lower left leg is horribly mangled; he is cold and will die soon if I cannot get the bleeding stopped.*

I seem to remember the time when a stable thrall was gored in the upper arm by a bull's horn. Father wrapped a leather strap around the arm and tied it tight enough to cut off the blood flow. The man lost his arm, but he lived. I have a leather thong in my shoulder bag. He tied it as tight as he could just below Lathan's knee. The blood flow slowed and finally stopped. *There, that should do,* Erik thought frantically to himself.

From their supplies, Erik quickly set up their tent and got a small oil lamp started. Then he set out some sleeping skins and got Lathan in and as comfortable as possible.

Shortly after the sun set, an eerie green light appeared over the tent. Lathan reached up and pulled the flap open so he could see out. The sky had cleared overhead, and unlike the previous night, the Northern Lights were spectacular. Green and purple waves that looked almost liquid shimmered across the sky. *I have never seen the lights like this in Norway. They never shine this brilliantly,* Erik thought.

"Really something out here, aren't they?" Lathan's weak voice was barely above a whisper.

"You're awake! It is good to hear your voice. Would you like some dried meat and water? The others should be here by mid-morning or so and we can get you back to the ship where you will be better cared for. I got the bleeding stopped at least." Erik sounded as cheerful as he dared.

"Maybe some water. Don't feel much like going anywhere right now. Those lights are something, aren't they?" Lathan sounded very weak.

"What are you saying? You will be back working the farm, your farm, by summer's end. I am glad you will finally be a Freeman." Erik tried his best to sound supportive.

"You? What do you know of me? We just met four months ago. You are just a blue-blood kid who thinks because you got high and mighty relatives, you naturally know how things are. You know nothing." Lathan knew he had little enough time to have his say.

"I have come out here on this ice so you could kill a bear. And what happens? You get yourself lost while the dogs I trained bring *your* bear to bay. By some joke of the gods, they get killed, my nephew who I raised as my own gets killed, and here I lay, dying. Keir, he was a good boy. He was a little slow, but he always meant well. You and your kind never gave him so much as a 'Thank you' or 'Good job.' He gladly shoveled your horseshit and never asked for anything. But your kind never even noticed he was there." Lathan seemed to be gathering strength from somewhere.

"I won't be going back to the ship. You see those lights up there? They are calling me. Ah, you think I am a lowly thrall and have no calling to Valhalla? You are wrong, and I can tell you why. First, I died in battle against a great ice bear enemy. And you are not the only blue-blood on this slab of ice. My mother was a thrall, a housemaid, sure enough. But my father—that is a whole other matter. You come across the sea, and all you know is Greenlanders are pathetic poor people. But you are wrong. My mother was a housemaid in Iceland before coming here. Your very uncle,

Sigurd, bedded her, and I am the result." He continued his tirade as Erik listened, feeling both insulted and ashamed.

"Thorkell knows, Haakon knows. Your father is more concerned with his own affairs to care, but he probably knows. He just never told you. At the Midsummer Festival this year, Thorkell's plan was to free me of obligations and give me a plot of land. Hah! He can save his land now. With me and the boy gone, he has nothing to feel guilty about now. For all these years, he never felt guilty enough to change my position."

"What are you saying? We are all Christians now. The Christ will heal you and get you back on your feet." Erik was starting to get desperate.

"Your Christian god has no place out here, boy. There's not a church for a thousand leagues. Erik the Red did not know any Christian gods. He knew the old gods and knew Greenland was made for them. Then Leif and his mother bring Christianity in like it was some great victory. This land is too wild for that. Erik knew that. He never slept with the woman after that, you know. No Christian god for Sigurd either. No Christian god made a fool of him; he wouldn't hear of it. I am my father's son."

Erik was tired and had a hard time staying awake while Lathan droned on. Erik did not have the energy for the Christianity vs. pagan gods debate. His adrenaline rush from the bear killing and the aftermath had worn off, and he was exhausted. He just wanted Lathan to fall asleep and wake up with some energy in the morning. Lathan's dialog slowed finally, and he seemed to go to sleep, or maybe Erik did.

CHAPTER 3
ERIK'S DREAM

E rik and Lathan were walking through a heath along a cart trail. It was well after sunset, and there was not a cloud in the dark sky. However, many of the stars were obscured by wavering curtains of green and purple.

"I have never seen the Lights shine so brilliantly!" Erik exclaimed.

"They generally do in these parts," Lathan retorted curtly.

Just over a rise, a haze of light, as if from a village, began to show. They walked toward the light without speaking, Lathan limping on a bad left leg. As they topped the hill they could see the source of the light. It was a great hall, with many rooms, all lit up. Glowing smoke belched from smoke holes along the roofline that seemed to go on and on in both directions. In the center was a great room. A huge wooden door was open a crack and brilliant light shone around it.

As they approached the hall, the path led through a small forest. Somehow Erik knew there were one hundred trees, each with one protruding limb twenty hands from the ground. A man was hanging by the neck, dead, from each tree. Each man looked like Lathan, with thick eyebrows, a broad nose, and coarse brown hair.

When they were still a few paces from the door, it swung open, and a wolf howled from inside. A long table became visible with a trench style fire pit lit up behind it. At the table sat many men and women. Great platters of food and horns of drink were set all along the table. In the central High Chair sat a large man with long, flowing gray hair and beard. Around his neck, laying against polished silver chainmail hung a large medallion with a great, gold, ornately engraved "O" on it. Gold arm bands encircled both his powerful upper arms.

On his right, in another ornately carved chair, sat another large man wearing a silver helmet that had lightning bolts of gold inlaid on each side. This man had dark-blond hair and beard. An intricately engraved silver and gold Thor's Hammer, Mjollnir, hung on a chain around his neck. The two big men were drinking from golden ram horn steins.

All up and down the table were men drinking and

laughing. Several had beautiful, blonde, young women on their laps. The table went on as far as Erik could see in both directions. Down the hall, in front of the great table were couples fornicating. Still farther were men locked in mortal combat with longswords or battle axes.

At one place down the table was a man mounted on what appeared to be a young woman. He was driving into her like one of Harald's stallions. She was locked onto him, her legs wrapped tightly around his thighs. Little rivulets of blood flowed from the scratches on his back from her fingernails. Her head was buried in his neck so that her face was not visible. The man's hair was long and flowing reddish-blond. It looked somehow familiar. The man went into a frenzy of hard, fast humping as the girl hung on and seemed to crave the assault, screaming in delight. Finally, he obviously spent himself in her. He turned and looked right at Erik—was it Uncle Sigurd? He had a triumphant smile on his rosy face with its thick orange beard. Then the girl looked at Lathan. She had long, mousy-brown, curly hair, and her face looked like Lathan's. Sweat poured from both, and she had a dreamy half-smile on her face. Her dark eyes looked right through Erik, then shifted to Lathan, who stood there trembling.

In another ornately carved chair on the king's left side sat a good-looking man with long, shiny black hair and dark, wild eyes. He was dressed in a hooded black robe. A silver chain hung around his neck with a stylish L-shaped medallion. The man looked right at Lathan. His head spun around and became a beautiful woman with long black hair and shiny black eyes. Suddenly she sprang onto the table wearing a wide smile and showing bright white teeth. She then became a huge black wolf with yellow eyes. The wolf leaped and attacked Lathan, devouring him in an instant. The man in the lightning bolt helmet stood up, grabbed something off the table, and hurled it at the wolf, killing it dead. From the Wolf's head stuck a large, ornately engraved silver and gold Thor's Hammer.

Erik stood in awe, not able to move or say anything. Presently, the wolf began to break up into wolf pups, each running in circles, yelping, finally running through the big door and into the hall. Shortly, the handsome black-haired man returned to the table and took his seat as if nothing had happened.

The king looked at Erik and reached his hand out, making a motion for Erik to come to the table. Scared, but not wanting a retribution, Erik started to follow the summons when a strange warmth and golden light began to glow from behind him. The light became stronger and warmer, spreading through his cold body. As it did, the king and the whole hall became smaller and dimmer. A soft and deep man's voice from some-

where behind Erik said, "You do not want this one, he is of no use to you."

A warm and peaceful sensation radiated through Erik's back.

CHAPTER 4
CONTACT

Peluk was up well before the sun. He relit his soapstone lamp and melted some snow in a cup, put in some dried seal meat and ground willow leaves, and made a small stew. He was ready before the sun rose above the horizon. With the new light he hoped he would be able to catch the bear soon. He prayed it had chosen to sleep. No new snow had fallen, but clouds were still visible in the southwest. Before sunrise he was able to follow the bear's bloody footprints. They led east and a little south.

After working around some ice blocks, he came to a large flat expanse. On the far side, maybe two hands of time walk away, he could see some dark specks. He headed that way, and when about a half a hand away, he could see a white lump with some darker colors around it. Near the white lump was what looked like a small tent. *How can it be? Who would beat me here? And where are they? The white lump may be the bear I seek, but it is dead, and now my brother's soul is lost for all time.* His eyes filled with tears again, and his throat felt tight.

As he approached, he could see that it was the site of a bear kill. But who was in this area to kill a bear? *Black Rock hunters?* As he got closer, he got a better picture of what might have happened. There was a small crescent-shaped lead that had frozen over in the night. On the far side, there was a bloody dog's body and another on the near side, probably killed by the bear. Neither looked like any dog or wolf he had ever seen. On the near side, toward the north end of the lead, there was a man's body sprawled as if had been attacked from behind by the bear. Near the small tent was a lot of blood. The bear was lying close to the tent. It had been wounded in the gut, lungs, and heart. He could tell by the colors of the frozen blood. A broken spear was still embedded deep in the animal's side. The rest of the broken shaft lay on the ice. It was made from a type of wood he did not recognize. The bear had been gutted, apparently only the heart had been eaten. No attempt to skin it had been started. The kill must have taken place shortly before dark. The footprints around the kill site told him the people who killed this bear were strangers. One had a badly wounded leg.

"Greetings!" Peluk said as confidently as he could, hoping someone in the little tent would answer. *The People have no material like that tent is made from. These must be the strangers who traded with the Black Rock Clan last spring. Where are they?*

Looking around, he spied a spear laying on the snow a short distance from the big bloodstain on the other side of the tent. The tip was made of iron shaped in a way he had never seen, and the shaft was of that same strange wood. *These strangers must come from a faraway land!*

With no one stirring, Peluk decided to get brave and lift the tent flap. In the dim light, he could tell there were two men in there. One seemed to be making slight quivering movements while the other was still. Peluk held his spear at the ready with his good hand while he carefully lifted a corner of the blanket with the crippled one. Two human shapes in caribou sleeping skins and caribou hide clothes lay there, both quite helpless. The one was obviously dead, his icy eyes staring at nothing, his body perfectly still with one leg a bloody mess below the knee. The other seemed to be unconscious and shivering uncontrollably. He knew he had to act fast.

Peluk put all of his sleeping skins over the live

man and prepared to build a fire. He had enough seal oil and a small soapstone lamp. He used his tent to make a shelter around the freezing man. Once he had a fire in his lamp, he arranged it so that the heat would enter the shelter. In a few heartbeats, he generated a spark into the willow catkins, and his fire was lit. Next, he used the catkin flame to ignite a wick made of some dried plant fiber twisted and soaked with seal fat and placed it in his lamp filled with hardened seal fat. The wick slowly ignited more of the wick material that had been pressed into the fat along an edge of the bowl-shaped lamp. All of the fat-soaked wick material ignited and soon was giving off some good heat. As soon as he had some warmth in the shelter, Peluk began to uncover the man to see who or what he was. First, he had to move the dead man. *Is this a man? It looks like a man but with dark, curled hair on its head and brown, curled hair on its face. It has arms and legs, hands and feet. No time to dwell on the dead.*

When he uncovered the live one, he was even more shocked to see the face his brother had told him White Rock described from one of her dreams! He had long yellow hair and fine straight hair on his cheeks and chin. His face was pale white, his lips were almost blue and his eyes were barely slits but looked blue. Gently, Peluk took the man's clothes off and noted that under the caribou outer clothes, he wore some sort of woven material that he could not identify. Then, he removed his own clothing and slid into the sleeping skins and pressed their naked bodies tightly together. Slowly he could feel the man's body begin to warm.

In about a hand of time, the man began to shiver violently. Peluk knew this was a good sign. Soon the man's eyes began to flutter, and he jerked awake. Not knowing what was happening, he began to struggle, but Peluk was stronger than the big man, even with his bad arm, and pinned the man's arms at his sides and held him tight. Soon he started talking weakly in some tongue Peluk could not understand. The look in his blue eyes was sheer terror. Peluk tried to talk calmly and reassure him that he needed to get warm before moving around, the man was not settling down, and it was sapping his own strength trying to restrain the man.

Light began to work its way into Erik's mind. He was being restrained, and something warm was plastered against his back. Scared, weak, and disoriented, he started thrashing around trying to get away from whatever had him captured. When the sleeping skins were tossed off, he realized he was naked, and so was a short, dark man. In his struggle to get free, Erik used up most of his strength and collapsed back onto the bedding. The other man had gotten off the skins and was putting his own clothes on. Something was odd about this man.

What is it? I cannot think...this is just a boy, no older than Sven...and he has a crippled arm. No wonder I could get away as weak as I am. He is a Skræling! Where is a weapon? Wait, I think he is trying to help me.

Erik was so weak; he could only look at the boy in the dim light of the small shelter. His body still trembled, and he could not comprehend what was happening. *Yet I do not think I am in danger from this Skræling.*

The boy held a small spear in his good arm pointed at him and then to his clothes with the shriveled one, motioning for Erik to get dressed. "Who are you? Where did you come from? Where are the others?" Erik demanded. The boy just looked at him and pointed to his clothes with the odd-looking spear. When he did start to get his clothes together, the boy put his spear down and smiled.

After he had Erik settled down, the stranger turned to some other task with his back toward Erik. *What is going on?* In a few minutes, the stranger turned and offered Erik a cup made from what he guessed was walrus skin that had some hot liquid in it. It was a tea that Erik could not identify. He took a small taste, surprised the taste was tolerable. A bit bitter, but Erik was dreadfully thirsty and even hungry. The tea felt good going down but churned in his stomach like it was not going to stay there. He tried to relax but found that impossible. He still did not know what was happening. Looking around, he could see they were under his tent. The only light was given off by an oily-smelling little bowl with some kind of animal fat burning. As his head began to clear, the more foul the place smelled. He lifted the closest edge of the flap and saw that the sun was bright and less than a hand above the southeastern horizon.

Suddenly Erik's memory started to engage. The bear, the dogs, Keir, Lathan...*Where is Lathan?* He began to panic again. "Where are we? What have you done with my friends?!" he shouted. In the dim light, Erik could see the boy look at him with curiosity in his eyes. He realized the youth had no understanding of what he was saying. He had to find a way to communicate somehow. Erik pointed to the caribou skin the boy had wrapped around him and said. "Blanket."

Peluk looked at the strange yellow-haired man and said, "That is a caribou hide from the summer hunting grounds of the People. It gave up its soul so that the People can stay alive through the winter and until the next turning of the seasons. Sister Caribou was honored at the time she was taken by a hunter of the People who was my brother. She was also honored by the members of the Seal Clan, led by Tunik at the fall equinox before the people settled into their winter homes. When the season turned to bring in the Awakening moon, the People moved to a hunting camp on the sea ice to hunt seals."

Erik thought, *What was all that about?* He shrugged his shoulders, then pointed to himself and slowly said, "Erik."

The dark-haired boy looked at him with a questioning look, then rattled off another long statement and pointed at Erik.

Erik looked back at him, raised his voice, and jabbed his thumb into his chest then said, "ERIK."

The stranger looked puzzled, then smiled as if he figured it out and jabbed his thumb into his own chest and said, "Urk!"

Erik shook his head, pointed to himself again and said slowly, "Erik."

Finally, the boy pointed at him and said. "Uruk?"

Erik thought to himself, *Close enough,* and gave the boy a smile and a big nod. The boy looked pleased with himself. Next Erik pointed at the boy and asked, "Your name?"

The boy looked puzzled, then smiled and rattled off a word or several of them that Erik could not begin to comprehend.

The boy pointed to Erik and said, "Uruk...?" asking a long-worded question.

Erik thought he needed to keep it simple. He pointed to the spear in the boy's lap and said, "Spear."

The boy grabbed it up and pointed it toward Erik and went into another long speech with a serious look on his face.

Erik took that as a threat. So he took the cup took a drink and said, "Good."

The boy smiled and ran off another long explanation.

Slowly Erik's fingers began to function, and he found he could wiggle his toes. The boy was warming his inner boots and stockings by the fire so that when he put them on his feet, they felt reasonably normal. It was somewhat awkward in the shelter where he only had enough room to sit up in. Then he reached for his outer caribou skin tunic, and the boy smiled, pointed and said "Parka."

Erik thought, *No, it's a tunic*, then he realized

the boy had a word for this called *parka*. Erik smiled and said, "Parka."

The boy smiled and nodded vigorously. The boy pointed to Erik's outer boots and said, "Mukluk."

Erik smiled and said, "boot."

The boy nodded and said, "Mukluk."

Erik said, "Mukluk," and they both smiled.

Next the boy reached into a bag and pulled out some dried meat and offered some to Erik. Erik thought it could not be worse than lutefisk, so he took the piece and bit into it. Again, his stomach started to churn, but he managed to keep it down. He figured it must be good for him out here on the ice. This boy came out of nowhere and saved him from freezing to death, which by now he figured must have been what happened to Lathan. After eating, Erik suddenly felt extremely tired. He laid back onto the pile of skins and pulled the top one over him. He figured one would be enough now that he had his clothes back on. His thoughts became confused again, and soon he drifted off to sleep.

The next thing Erik knew, it was warmer in the shelter, and the boy was not in the tent. He crawled out of the shelter and stood up. It was strange to be on his feet. His muscles were sore and his balance unsteady. It hurt his feet to stand, and it was much worse when he tried to walk. His hands ached, and he still had little control of his fingers.

The boy, who now Erik could see was at least three hands shorter than he and appeared to be about three or four years younger. *Sven could never do the things this boy is doing. I couldn't either at his age,* he admitted to himself.

The Skræling boy reached into a sealskin bag he carried on his good shoulder and pulled out a pair of big skin mittens and handed them to Erik, motioning him to put them on. Carefully, Erik slid them on. They were made of ice bear skin with the hair inside. Cold at first, they quickly warmed, which made his hands ache even more. But soon enough he could move his fingers and feel his strength returning to his hands.

Erik looked around. The first thing he saw was Lathan's frozen body. It was a grizzly sight. He took a wool blanket from the tent and dragged it over Lathan's body. Then he took in the rest of the scene. Some snow flurries or blown snow had covered the site with a light dusting. Still visible was Keir's broken body, Vigi and Floki's frozen corpses, and the bloodied bear. *How many days ago was it?* He had no idea. His mind drifted to that day as he recalled the events as they unfolded.

Erik's new "friend" was walking over to him.

When he got next to Erik and looked up, he smiled and said, "Uruk." Then he went on with a bunch of words Erik could not understand.

The boy looked at the bear, shook his head, and said something to himself. Then he kneeled down and looked at the damaged paw and said something else. Next, he looked off to the west with a faraway look in his eye. *Did this boy know this bear? Was he hunting him and that is how he happened to find me?*

The boy reverently looked into the bear's face, put his hand on the bear's head, and chanted something, almost a song. Then he looked at the bear's fatal wound. He looked up at Erik, pointed at the wound and asked, "Uruk?"

Erik nodded.

The youth got up and took Erik's hand and uttered a long diatribe that completely mystified Erik. Some of it sounded almost reverent, some wistful, some scornful, even hateful. Tears filled the boy's eyes. Erik could only shrug and slowly pulled his hand away. He had no concept of what the boy was trying to communicate.

Erik decided again to try to get this strange boy's name. He pointed to himself and said, "Erik" then pointed to the Skræling and put his hands up in a questioning manner.

The boy said something that went on for

several heartbeats, but Erik thought he caught a sound he could manage '...*Peluk*...' So he pointed to the boy and said "Peluk."

The boy looked thoughtful for a moment, nodded his head vigorously, and said "Peluk" as he pointed to himself. Their pronunciation was not exactly the same, but at least they had names to call each other. Erik was glad that he finally had a name for this strange boy.

Erik pointed to Lathan's body and said, "Lathan."

Peluk became upset and shook his head vigorously, pointing to his mouth closed tight. Erik did not understand and started to repeat Lathan's name, but Peluk put his hand to Erik's mouth and shook his head vehemently. Erik began to understand—do not say a dead man's name. *Must have something to do with evil spirits and dead people.* Peluk pointed to himself, then Erik, and said a word that Erik took to mean friend or acquaintance maybe. Then he pointed to Erik, then Lathan's body, and said the same word. Erik got the meaning and repeated the word with some difficulty. Peluk smiled and nodded rapidly.

Peluk grabbed Erik by the arm and pulled. Erik pulled back, suddenly feeling threatened. Peluk smiled and patted Erik on the shoulder and made a gesture that Erik took to mean that he was getting his strength back. That made Erik truly believe that Peluk cared about his well-being. He wanted to prove he was grateful for Peluk saving his life. As he surveyed their location, he spotted Keir's spear laying across the lead. He walked around to retrieve the spear as a gift to Peluk.

Just as he broke the spear loose from the snow-pack, he heard Peluk yelling, "Uruk, Uruk!"

Erik looked up to see Peluk standing on the large ice block by the camp and pointing to the south-southeast. Erik looked but could not see anything, so he ran back to where Peluk was and climbed up on the ice block. By the time he was in place, he was winded and felt weak in the knees. His strength was not all back yet.

Looking in the direction Peluk pointed, Erik was blinded by the bright whiteness of everything in his view reflecting the sun, which was now just past its peak. Peluk had a small flat piece of antler tied on his face with slits cut at the eyes that cut down on the glare. The piece was cut slender and rounded so that it fit face profiles comfortably, especially for Peluk whose face was broader and flatter than Erik's.

Seeing that Erik had no eye protection, Peluk reached into a bag he carried and pulled out a similar device for Erik to use. Erik tied the rawhide strings behind his head and looked through the slits. The device did not fit Erik as well as it did Peluk, but the effect was remarkable. It did not make everything clear, but it helped tremendously. Now on careful inspection, he could make out several dark specks far to the southeast, and they appeared to be moving toward their campsite. Erik thought *wolves*, but then he could make out that most were on two feet. He realized it must be Haakon's men. *I will be saved!*

But what about Peluk? My countrymen will not see a Skræling as anything but a threat and kill him for sure. I must convince Peluk to leave immediately. He pointed to the figures, then to himself, then to himself and to the figures, then motioned that he and them were together. He said, "Peluk must go, now!" and pointed west. Peluk just shook his head, not understanding.

Erik quickly hurried back to the shelter and started folding the sleeping skins, then pulled the canvas cover off the tent poles. Peluk caught on and set to work packing up what was left.

Erik interrupted his new friend's work and gestured to the west saying, "Peluk go!" Erik held out the spear to Peluk, pointed to himself and said "Erik," then pointed to the spear and pushed it to Peluk and said, "Peluk." Peluk seemed to understand the meaning of the gift. Erik then went to his own hunting bag and pulled out a piece of sandstone. He quickly showed Peluk how to slide the sandstone over the spear point to keep it sharp. Peluk caught onto that quickly. Then Erik pulled out a piece of rabbit skin that had been soaked in fat. He wrapped the skin around the spear point and tried to explain it would keep it from rusting. Peluk shrugged his shoulders and kept the point wrapped in the rabbit skin.

Peluk pointed to the west and said, "Uruk."

Erik shook his head vehemently. He pointed to the southeast, made a circle motion, then said, "Peluk," and made a slashing motion across his neck. Peluk seemed to get the idea that those men coming this way might kill him.

Peluk reached into his bag and pulled out a piece of walrus tusk shaped like a swimming seal with an odd human face carved into its belly. With a tear in his eye, he handed it to Erik, then wrapped his good arm around him and laid his head on Erik's chest while patting him on the back several times. Erik responded by patting Peluk on the back as well. Then Peluk just stood there and stared at the approaching men.

Erik was highly impressed with Peluk's skills and did not want any harm to come to him. But now he could see Haakon's men were too close for Peluk to get away.

Erik was truly concerned about Peluk's safety.

For the first time, he looked closely at his new friend and noticed that he had strange tattoos on his face. Maybe he could convince the Norsemen that Peluk was some sort of mystical healer and must be spared. He climbed up on the ice block and looked out for the approaching Norsemen. They were coming as straight for his position as they could while maneuvering around the scattered ice blocks. He could see now that there were eight men and three dogs.

The dogs had scented the camp some time earlier and were homed in on the odor of death and humans. The men were pulling a sledge while the dogs led the way, straining at their traces and barking excitedly. When a man holding a leashed dog some two hundred paces away rounded an ice block, Erik waved at them and got a response. *I will get back home*, he sighed to himself. He turned and looked at Peluk. The boy now had a worried look on his face.

By the time the Norsemen began to arrive, little more than a hand of time remained until sunset. They had left the ship at daylight that morning, and now it was late afternoon. They could not get back to the ship before nightfall.

Olaf was among the men from the ship. He told Erik they could find a track once in a while in some protected area between ice blocks so they knew they were coming the right way. Then, sometime after starting out, the dogs began to pick up scent. They weren't sure if it was Lathan's party, but the way the dogs were acting, it did not seem like another bear or seal. They had placed marker poles on their trail north so they could find their way back to the ship faster. The ice shelf was beginning to break up so the ship might be closer when they returned. They shared the feeling that this season seems to be unusually warm, so the break-up is coming fast this year.

———————

ERIK TOLD them of the disastrous encounter with the bear, Keir and Lathan's deaths, as well as the three dogs. How Lathan lost so much blood, he had frozen to death in the night, even in the small tent. Then, how Erik would have succumbed to the cold were it not for being found by a lone Skræling boy who nursed him back to health. How the boy was not a savage and really cared that Erik recovered.

He told the crew about the difficulties with communication, but they managed. Maybe the Skræling were not that bad after all. They laughed and guffawed, saying the Skræling was fattening him up so he could take a fat prize back to his village to be eaten. His animal friends would treat him like a hero.

Erik tried to defend Peluk, pointing out how he was prepared for anything and had skills that were perfect for life out here on the ice. They could not communicate well enough to talk about families or their homes, but the Skræling had a strange way of always turning his attention to the west, like he was homesick. He must belong to some special society because he had strange tattoos on his face, forehead, shoulders, and forearms. The message he got back was that they are mere savages living here because no one else wanted to, and at the first chance, they would shoot a poison arrow into him. Erik thought, *I have not seen a bow or arrows among Peluk's things. But then, with his crippled arm, it would not be possible for him to use a bow.*

The Norsemen looked at Peluk with hate and mistrust in their eyes. Until that moment, he had been standing close behind Erik, but as he stepped aside, they could see that he was just a boy, and with a crippled arm at that. They all laughed and said, "Hah, just a boy! He won't even make a good thrall—he only has one good arm!" Erik knew Peluk could hear the derision in their voices and could see he trembled in fear. He cowered closer to Erik.

Erik spoke to all, "Peluk here has great skills as

a healer. If we treat him with honor, I think he will lead us to his village where we can trade for walrus ivory and many skins of exotic animals we will find a great market for back home. He will help us in meeting and trading with his people." Erik hoped he was telling the truth.

"A few days past, you bragged you would kill any Skræling you met up with," Olaf scoffed. "What has changed your mind so completely?"

"From out of nowhere, this boy found me as I lay freezing to death and brought me back to good health. There is good in him and, I now think, in his people. I think if we respect them, they will trust us and become good trading partners," Erik tried to sound confident.

Bjarni, the group's leader said, "All right, we will bring the Skræling boy with us and he can lead us to his village. But the slightest trouble, and he is the first to feel cold steel. If we just let him go, we could be walking into a trap. Get that bear skinned and cut up. First light, we head back to the ship. Erik, do not let your little *friend* out of your sight."

CHAPTER 5
ABOARD HAAKON'S SHIP

They packed Keir and Lathan's frozen bodies and the bear skin with skull and paws attached. Erik took Lathan's spear and was reprimanded for giving a Skræling Keir's. Erik said he owed Peluk for saving his life, and a spear was little enough payment for that. Bjarni declared that no Skræling would be allowed to have a weapon like that. Erik would have to take it back from him, no questions asked.

Erik turned and said, "Peluk, I must have the spear back," as he pointed to it.

Peluk knew that he had become a slave and would have to endure whatever hardships were bestowed on him. He could convince Uruk to let him return to his people, but these others were too big, too rough to argue with. He would bide his time and escape when no one was watching. He handed the spear over to Uruk without an argument. As he did so, he noticed three men holding wicked-looking weapons made from wood and string. Each had a small spear attached to the string which was pulled back from the wood in a way that would send the small spear with its iron point right into his body. He wanted no part of that.

When Uruk took the big spear, the three relaxed the strings on the wood and took the small spears and put them into pouches on their backs. He smiled as bravely as he could. Then Uruk reached into his bag and pulled out the walrus tusk carving he had given him and held it toward him. *I cannot take back a gift—evil spirits will visit me.* He curled Uruk's fingers around it and pushed it back while he pointed to his chest, then to Uruk's. The man understood, but then another of the big men stepped in and said something loud as a question to Uruk, smiling all the time. Others joined in the shouting and laughed loudly. Uruk's face turned red, and he looked down as if he were ashamed. He looked at Peluk and kind of shrugged his shoulders—there was no smile. Now Peluk *was* worried.

He pointed to the west, then to himself, then west again. Uruk shook his head and pointed around at the others, then to him, then to the south. *No, I cannot go with Uruk. I must get back to my brother's body and tend to it. He must be returned to the Clan. I must get back to the Clan. Mukmanu-meet will skin me now for being gone so long. The ice will break up soon. The Clan is probably waiting for me to return so we can move back to the beach.* He pointed to himself and back to the west again as he reached for his shoulder bag. One of the big men came over and stepped on the bag so Peluk could not pick it up.

Peluk slowly looked up at the man, a tear ran down his cheek—not for himself; he cried for his brother's lost soul. The man grabbed his hood and shoved him toward the group, who were now standing in a semicircle waiting for Peluk to make the next move. The three with the wicked weapons put the little spears back in them and pointed them at him. Uruk put his hands up and rushed to get between Peluk and the men. He was shouting, almost pleading with them to stop. Slowly they lowered the weapons.

"What are you doing?" Erik shouted. "This boy can be our guide and help us in trading with the Skræling. He is harmless, look at him. He is afraid as a rabbit in a fox's den. We must convince him we need his help to deal with his people. If we keep it friendly, we will be better off. Let me talk with him, calm him down and convince him to come with us to show us his village. I am sure they are skilled hunters and have valuable skins and walrus ivory we can get for a small price."

Bjarni cut in, "You better talk fast—there is a storm brewing, and we need to get back to the ship. Convince him now, or we will have to tie him up and carry him."

Erik turned to him and said, "Peluk, come with us." As he waved around the group, including him, and pointed to the southeast where the crew had come from. The wind was beginning to blow harder, swinging to the northeast. Peluk realized he had no choice and slowly nodded.

———

"Good, let's get moving. That storm is coming in fast. We can get to the ship in two hands of time if we push it. Now let's go!" Bjarni said authoritatively as he grabbed a tow rope on the sled. Other men took the other ropes, and they started the journey back to the ship.

Growing weary from towing the heavy sledge, men were becoming disgruntled with the pace Bjarni was setting. "You push too hard. We are becoming weary. We need to stop, rest, eat!" complained a disgruntled Gunnar Svensson as he dropped the tow rope and stood defiantly facing Bjarni.

"Erik, pick up that tow rope. Let the Skræling stay here with Gunnar if he wishes," Bjarni stated and began moving again.

Erik stepped forward and grabbed the rope. Peluk was right on his heels. Gunnar stood still until the group moved past him without a word. When he realized he was being left behind, he quickly caught up, mumbling under his breath, "This is insane."

"Look! There is the ship!" Olaf exclaimed just a short while later.

Just above the southeast horizon of ice, the ship's banner at the top of the mast could be seen waving in the northeasterly wind. It had taken just under two hands of time to reach the ship.

Gunnar walked up and snatched the tow rope from Erik, saying, "Give me that! Go tend to your Skræling puppy." His tone was more of a snarl than words.

All of the men picked up their pace and moved with renewed energy. The ship had indeed been able to move farther north as the leading edge of the ice was breaking off and drifting southeast-ward on a strong current toward the sea.

In a few more steps, Peluk beheld the big knorr. It looked something like a canoe but was huge.

That is the biggest thing made by man that Peluk has ever laid eyes on! It is bigger than the Black Rock shaman's longhouse. Where did all the wood it is made of come from? How can it be? The big ship bobbed up and down with the waves, yet it was tied to the ice by two long lines that led out onto the ice and were tied to iron stakes driven into the surface ice. A large man with gray-streaked yellow hair on his face and flowing from under a wolf skin hat down over his big shoulders was yelling at men still on the big canoe and pointing to the band approaching. In a heartbeat, more men dressed in caribou parkas, leggings, and mukluks jumped from the great canoe and ran toward them. Intense fear strangled him as he burrowed into Uruk's back.

As they approached the ship, new men relieved their tired arms, legs, and backs, taking the tow ropes from the pullers and dragging the sledge to the side of the ship. They began unloading immediately. The first things taken were the bodies of Lathan and Keir. Haakon looked coldly at a healthy Erik and said, "I will want the whole story when there is time." Erik nodded and felt ashamed. Haakon then yelled, "Get these things aboard and ready to sail, a storm is coming in, and we have no shelter here!" To the west, the sky was filled with billowing storm clouds.

In less than a hand of time, they were under

way. Big men were pulling long paddles that pushed the big canoe through the water. The big man who seemed to be in charge was holding a piece of wood connected to another piece that reached down into the water. When he moved the wood in his hands one way, the canoe moved the opposite way, and when he moved it the other way, the canoe moved back the original way. Peluk was amazed.

The big man commanded Uruk and Peluk to sit next to him, and the man talked with Uruk. Peluk could understand from the way Uruk moved his hands that he talked of the bear and how he managed to kill it. His friend became very quiet, and his eyes flowed with tears when he talked of the men that were killed. Thinking of the dead men, Peluk recalled one's face looked about the same age as Uruk, the other, a little older (maybe an uncle to the younger one).

Uruk then pointed to Peluk and said many words. Among those words he made out "Peluk," "parka," and a few other words understood by both Uruk and Peluk. The big man, who Uruk called "Hukun," or something similar, studied Peluk with great interest.

The whole talk was continuously interrupted by someone up in the front of the canoe yelling something to Hukun. Each time he would move the wood in his hands, and the canoe would change directions. Peluk finally caught on that the man was warning Hukun about ice, and he was steering the canoe around it. They appeared to be moving south to get out of the current pushing ice along parallel to the sea ice. Peluk had never been this far from home nor this far from the ice pack. The dread and fear was building in him. There was much more ice flowing in this current than there should be this time of year. And now the waves were getting bigger as the storm was closing from the west, the direction of home.

Soon the sky became overcast, and the strong east wind caused Haakon to order the sail be lowered. They would have to keep moving south to get out of the flowing ice blocks, but they would have to do it with the oars rather than the sail. When they cleared the heaviest of the floating ice, Haakon changed direction to put the bow into the wind as it swung abruptly to the southwest so the heavy ship would ride the waves in a more stable manner. Rain began to slice through the air. To everyone's surprise, the rain was not freezing but almost tolerable. The winds whipped into a gale, however, and the waves became enormous. Controlling the ship foreshadowed talking about the Skræling with his nephew as Haakon concentrated on keeping the ship pointed into the waves.

Riding up and over the big waves, then down into the troughs, the big canoe jerking this way, then that, lunging forward then slowing down, then back up and over was something Peluk had never experienced. He soon found himself clutching the gunwale behind Hukun and retching his insides out over the side. He was becoming weak from such a sickness as he had never known. His good arm was starting to give out, and he was afraid he would be thrown over the side when Uruk came over and tied him tightly to the rail just below the side of the canoe. He nodded a thank you to Uruk just as his stomach erupted again.

CHAPTER 6
HAAKON BATTLES A STORM

Haakon fought the steerboard hard to keep the ship plowing into the waves. It was a rough ride, twisting, jerking, riding up and down over the waves like a log rolling through a set of rapids on a river. He prayed to the Almighty and, just to be safe, the pagan gods that *The Sea Mare* would hold together. They had managed to get south of the flowing ice chunks so he was less worried about colliding with a large ice block. He had six pairs of rowers working hard to help keep the ship on a course into the wind, though he knew they were not advancing across the sea—between the howling gale, darkness, and the current rushing toward the ocean, they would be lucky if they stayed close to one place. He had all other available hands baling water from below the deck because they were taking on a lot of spray over the gunwales. It was unnerving having the young Skræling right behind him heaving his guts out over the side.

Just before all light was lost, the sky began to lighten, and the rain began to slacken. The worst lightning moved on. At some point in the middle of the night, the storm had passed and stars could be seen through the thinning clouds. The wind continued to howl out of the west until nearly dawn. With the danger lessened Haakon put Bjarni in charge of the steerboard and crawled into his sleeping skins.

The dawn found the wind down to a mere breeze, clear skies, calming seas, and unusually warm air. When the seas calmed, before the dawn, a tired Erik tended to his young Skræling friend. Peluk's stomach had calmed, but he was exhausted, dehydrated, and weak. Erik tried to help him climb below the deck to get some food and water, but he refused, obviously terrified about going below the deck.

Peluk was determined to huddle in the little triangle area behind the steerboard where he had stayed during the storm. His back and ribs were bruised from being tied to and battered against the boat's rail. His mouth felt like the aftermath of a walrus fight, and his stomach felt like rotting seal guts. The water Erik gave him felt good in his mouth and going down his throat.

"That's it, drink. You will feel better," Uruk said in a calm voice to Peluk.

Uruk swished the drinking horn, showing what was in it and said, "Vatn."

Peluk looked at it and shrugged like he did not understand.

Uruk swished the horn again and repeated, "Vatn," very slowly.

Peluk looked at Uruk, then at the horn and repeated his word for "Water."

Uruk smiled and nodded his head vigorously. Peluk smiled and took the horn, saying "water," and drank it down.

Uruk nodded again and said, "Ja!"

Peluk looked puzzled and shook his head, handed Uruk the drinking horn, and said "Vatn..." adding a string of sounds Erik could not comprehend. Erik and Peluk spent the entire morning learning each other's words.

———

LATE IN THE MORNING, Haakon came up on deck and noted the ship still had the sail stowed and was just drifting in the calm water. Bjarni was fast asleep next to the steerboard. Only a few men were awake. They were looking for floating ice or just talking. Haakon looked at Erik and Peluk and said to Erik, "Why are we just sitting here? Has that little bastard told you anything of use yet? Where is his village? Can we get ivory and skins there? Does he even talk?"

"We have been trying to learn how to talk to each other. I think he knows a great many things, but his language is very difficult, and I am sure he thinks ours is too," Erik replied guardedly.

"Well, nephew, we don't have all summer to make a trade and get back to Norway. We will need to get Lathan's body back to Thorkell before it gets too ripe. That block of ice we have the bodies on will surely melt before we get back to Thorkell's hall if this warm weather holds.

"Find out if your little friend can get us to his village. I will get the rest moving," Haakon said calmly. Then he yelled, "Everybody up! Get this ship ready to move! We can't lay here all summer! Get a move on! I want six oars in the water and ready to hoist the sail in five minutes!"

He took the steerboard from Bjarni, and the big warrior stretched his back, made some circular motions with his arms, then stepped over and drained his water over the side while he yawned. Then he took a seat on the closest bench, grabbed an oar from the rack in the center of the deck and slid it through the oar port for his rowing position and awaited further orders. All this he did smoothly without uttering a word. Soon, twelve rowers, two to an oar, were in place with their oars sticking out the sides of the boat ready to get the ship moving. Four others grabbed ropes that would hoist the sail arm up the mast. Still others took the ropes that would be used to guide the sail once it was hoisted into place.

Haakon looked at Erik. "Where is his home?"

Erik looked into Peluk's eyes with an expression that said, "*Pay close attention and answer me what I ask you.*" Peluk gave a little nod, hoping he could understand.

Peluk worried that if he could not understand, these big men would make sure he never saw his family again.

Uruk pointed to Peluk, swung his arm in a wide arc, and said, "Peluk, where is your home?"

Peluk blinked a few times trying to figure out what Uruk was asking. He thought, *maybe he is asking if Peluk knows the sea to the north. Maybe they are going to take me home. I am sure Tunik had guided the rest of the Clan back to the beach by now. Tunik and Mukmanumeet surely would have known that a storm was coming and moved the people to their village safely before it struck. Since Peluk has never been this far from home, I cannot say that I know where the village is from here. But I think if they can move the canoe back to the north and west, the line of sea ice would take us home.*

He looked at the sun, rolled his eyes while he thought, then pointed toward the northwest and said, "The homelands of the Seal Clan are that way from here."

Uruk smiled and patted him on the back.

"Northwest from here, Uncle," Erik said in a triumphant voice.

"I knew that, Erik. How far—how many days?" Haakon demanded.

Again, Uruk looked into Peluk's black eyes and said, "Can Peluk tell Erik how many days to Peluk's home village?" He pointed to the sun, then traced a line through the sky to the west to the horizon, kept the circle going until he hit the eastern horizon and traced back to the late morning sun.

Peluk thought for a few minutes then he traced the same line. He nodded his head and said a word in his guttural language and smiled. He knew what Uruk was asking—what do the people call a day? He was proud of himself until he looked at Hukun who looked anything but happy. He sheepishly looked back at Erik.

Erik made the same motion and said, "Day."

Peluk smiled and said, "Daag."

Then Erik pointed to Peluk, made the motion,

said "Dagr," then he counted on his fingers, "One, two, three? How many?"

Peluk looked puzzled and stared out across the open water. *Only an occasional chunk of ice can be seen from here. How do I tell them I do not know how far it is? I cannot see any ice or land to make a judgment.* Finally, he looked at Uruk and shrugged his shoulders. He waved across the sea and said, in his own tongue, that he did not know exactly where the village lies. *When we get close enough to see land, I will know. I pray Hukun will not kill me for my lack of information.*

When Erik relayed to Haakon that Peluk does not know how far, only the general direction, Haakon took a deep breath and shouted, "Northwest we go; this better be a short trip. Surely that kid cannot be very far from his home. He has no horse, no boat, no way to travel very far. We'll see if he recognizes anything by day's end." He grabbed the steerboard and ordered the sail trimmed so they traveled west by northwest.

In a hand of time, they began to see ice flowing toward the east. Haakon stayed on the south side of the floating ice. He ordered Erik and Peluk to the front of the ship so Peluk could see anything he knew and could pass information on through Erik. Haakon knew that Erik was the only one on the ship that Peluk trusted.

Just as the sun was almost to the horizon, Peluk pointed toward the sun and yelled in his language "Land, Land!" He was obviously very excited to sight his homeland. But several of the Norsemen thought perhaps he was too jubilant, and wondered if there was an ambush planned ahead.

Haakon looked at the sliver of land visible along the horizon and smiled. *The little Skræling knows his directions, I'll give him that,* he mused to himself. "We will be close enough to land tomorrow. Lower the sail, and we will get some rest in this area tonight. Four rowers will keep the ship close to where we are. Everyone else, get some sleep. We need to be on our toes tomorrow."

Before first light, Haakon had everyone in position to set sail for the land they spotted the previous evening. The four rowers were ordered to get some sleep while the ship moved toward the land. As the day dawned, the flowing ice was visible off the steerboard side of the ship, and the land was straight ahead but still just a sliver on the western horizon. It appeared there was more mountainous land on the south side of the place the Skræling pointed to. But when they got closer it became evident there were two land masses separated by a channel. Much of the flowing ice was streaming through that channel. Vegetation could be seen on the southern land while the northern land was still covered with ice and snow. Peluk was pointing to the northern land mass, so it was assumed his home was over there. It was apparent now that they could maneuver through the ice flow and end up in open water before they arrived at a gravel beach.

CHAPTER 7
SEAL CLAN VILLAGE

E rik watched as Peluk studied the shore carefully. He began to get a worried look on his face and kept studying the land. Now and then he would look to the east and have a puzzled expression. Eventually it dawned on Erik that the odd-looking clumps of rocks on the beach near the cliffs were low houses or huts. There were no people and no smoke rising from any of the structures. Peluk was increasingly nervous and agitated. Tears began to form in his eyes. Finally, the keel of the ship slid onto gravel. Erik had decided some time ago that the village looked deserted. He also knew the tide was going out, and it would be most of the day before they would be able to set sail again.

As soon as he was able, Peluk jumped from the ship, landing in waist-deep water. Erik was right behind him as he bolted for the village. The men shouted to Erik, "Do not follow him, it might be a trap!" Erik ignored them because he could see how upset Peluk was becoming.

The first house they arrived at was bigger than most of the others. Peluk disappeared into a tunnel that came out on the east side of the house. As he entered he was shouting, "Tunik! Tunik! Muku-keet! Mukukeet!"

Erik did not follow, nor did he know what the words meant. Soon Peluk came back out the way he went in. Tears filled his eyes and ran down his cheeks. He looked panicked. He ran from house to house yelling and crying. Finally, he threw up his good arm and let out a blood-curdling scream of "EIY-EEEEEE!!!!" The men on the ship put arrows in their bows, readying for an attack, but soon noticed it was just Peluk wandering around in circles screaming.

Erik tried to approach him, but he ran away up a trail leading up the cliff. The trail was still clogged with snow and ice, and Peluk had diffi-culty climbing. Erik wanted to help him, get him calmed down, but did not know how. Finally, Peluk came out on a rock ledge about thirty hands above the beach. He was looking out over the sea.

He obviously spotted something off to the north. All Erik saw was beach and mud flats left by the receding tide. Peluk slid down the steep trail and bolted to the north up the beach. Erik ran after him. He could not help but admire how quickly Peluk could run on the cobblestone and gravel beach.

After running a couple hundred paces up the beach, Peluk turned out onto the mud flat. There, some hundred paces out, was a gray clump of something Peluk seemed to be struggling to reach. The gooey mud was most difficult to trudge through. Soon it was up to Peluk's knees, but he struggled on until he reached the mass and started desperately trying to roll it over. At last Erik realized it was a body.

"Grandmother!" Peluk screamed.

He recognized her parka but was not able to get her rolled over. Suddenly he realized a huffing and puffing Uruk was by him. Uruk reached down into the mud and rolled the old woman over with ease. Her face was swollen and bleached white from being in the water for some time. Her clothes were saturated and heavy.

"How did you get here?" Peluk cried. "And where are the others?" *Surely Tunik is close by, isn't he? Oh Grandmother, what has happened? What*

terrible thing? Evil spirits have been at play!
"EIYEEEEE!!!!!!!!!!!!!!"

He turned to Erik. "They are gone...all gone."
He waved his arm out over the sea. "They must
have been still on the ice when the storm came.
Evil spirits drove the storm." He hugged the old
woman and looked forlornly toward the village,
knowing he could never get her there by himself.
He gave Erik a pleading look.

Erik bent over and picked the soggy, muddy
mess up, put her over his shoulder, and asked,
"Where?" Peluk understood and pointed toward
the village. Erik slogged his way back onto the
gravelly beach and headed back toward the village.
Peluk led the way and kept checking on Erik's
progress as they made their way back.

Behind the bigger house, Peluk showed Erik a
small pool of clean water and motioned for him to
put her in there. Peluk then lovingly and thor-
oughly cleaned the mud from her. With help from
Erik, he undressed her and cleaned her whole
body. He washed her caribou calfskin dress and
leggings, then her sealskin boots and carefully set
them out on the rocks to dry. It was obvious she
was someone Peluk knew, probably a
grandmother.

After that, Peluk hurried into the first house he

had entered when they arrived at the village. He emerged from the tunnel in a short period of time and hurried over to another large structure.

Erik noted the walls of these houses were rocks piled in a kind of circle or oval with a tunnel leading out on one side. Most of the tunnels pointed east. He was curious but felt he should not go into any of the structures.

Peluk returned after a bit longer in that house. He had a strange looking, shaved sealskin bag slung over his good shoulder. The bag had mystical-looking designs made from shell beadwork on the outside of the flap.

Peluk went back to the old woman's body. Her skin was shriveling and turning darker already. Peluk implored Erik to help him put the clothing back on her. The day was warm and dry with a bright sun so that her clothes were only damp now. They got her dressed, then Peluk signaled for Erik to pick her up again.

He led Erik to a rock face in a sharp gully that had formed in the cliff behind the village. Peluk pointed to a rock ledge that had been formed long ago when the sea level was much higher. Peluk struggled but soon made his way up to the ledge and motioned for Erik to bring the old woman. With some difficulty, Erik managed to get her up there. The ledge was something like a cave and was completely protected from the elements. The floor was smooth and dry, and the opening was high enough to kneel but not stand. It went back about a man's height into the dark gray rock, tapering to a solid wall. It went on about three body lengths to the west. Across the gully, Erik noted a matching ledge, but it had ice on it while this south side was quite dry.

Peluk put the shoulder bag down and took out a finely tanned caribou hide blanket. He carefully laid it out so that it had no wrinkles in it, hair side up. Then he motioned for Erik to help him lay the body out on her back.

Next he reached into the bag and pulled out a crystal amulet attached to what appeared to be a necklace of braided black human-hair. He gently lifted her head and slipped the necklace around her neck, placing the amulet on her chest. Erik noticed it was a seal's head with human facial features. It was exquisitely crafted.

Again, Peluk reached into the bag and pulled out a mask. It depicted the same kind of seal head with a human face. The mouth was a straight line, neither smiling nor frowning. Peluk gently laid it on the old woman's face.

Next, he pulled from the bag an ivory talisman. It was about a finger and a half long and depicted a seal in a laid-out position like it was swimming. Other than the seal face and the flippers it was covered with at least twenty carved small human faces. Some were smiling, some appeared to be sad or crying, a few had an angry look. Some had their mouths in an "O" shape with big eyes. One had features similar to a bear's face with big fangs. Many had oversized ears. Erik certainly had never seen anything like it. Peluk folded the old woman's arms into an "X" over her chest and placed the talisman in her hand and gently wrapped her fingers around it.

Next, Peluk pulled out a small drum and drumstick. The drum was no bigger than the palm of Erik's hand. Finally, the youth pulled out a raven wing, what looked like a falcon's wing, a small leather pouch, and another seal/human mask.

This mask he placed over his own face and slid a thong over his head to hold it in place. Peluk put two fingers into the pouch and produced a yellowish powder, which he sprinkled over the woman's chest. Next, he picked up the drum in his deformed hand and tapped on the skin with the little drumstick in his good hand. As he did that he chanted what Erik took as a prayer. After a short time, he carefully put the drum and drumstick down. With his good hand he picked up the raven wing and waved it over the woman's head reciting a different chant, then ceremoniously set the raven wing down and picked up the falcon wing. This he made a kind of flying motion with, his head held up like he was looking toward the heavens. With the mask on, Erik could not tell if his eyes were closed or open. He started yet another chant, starting with low notes, then ascending as he flapped the wing higher over the woman. When he finished, he reverently put the wing down and slipped the mask off his face. He looked longingly at the woman, tears filling his eyes. Finally, he carefully put the things back in the bag. He left the first mask, the amulet, and the talisman with the woman and motioned for Erik to head back.

Erik reached the ground, turned and helped Peluk back down. As they started down the gully trail back toward the village, Erik heard Gunnar yelling, "Erik, you all right? The little bastard didn't gut ya, did he?"

"All is fine here, Gunnar," Erik yelled back.

Peluk looked at Erik with a puzzled and worried face. Tears still streaked down his cheeks.

Erik understood that Peluk had lost his whole family, all his friends, and possibly every person he ever knew until he found Erik freezing in that little tent. How horrible he must feel. Yet he had the strength to conduct that very touching funeral for his grandmother. Erik wondered why he would do that. No one was there, no one would ever know. Was the funeral really for his whole family, his whole village? Maybe one day Peluk would be able to tell him.

When they neared the village, Peluk noticed several Norsemen carrying things from the village to the ship. He panicked and ran toward them yelling, *"Nienn! Nienn!"*—a Norse word he had learned from Erik.

"Norse must not take these things! They belong to the People!" Peluk shouted as he stepped in front of a wiry-built warrior. His movement was so swift that it startled the man who quickly dropped the bundle of tanned caribou hides he was carrying.

Thinking he was being attacked by Skræling, a fear all the Norsemen shared, Tyrkir pulled the axe from his belt and slammed it into Peluk's head. Blood sprayed everywhere as Peluk slumped to the ground, briefly jerked, then lay still, his dead eyes staring in disbelief.

"NOOOOOO!!!!" Erik screamed as he ran to catch up with Peluk.

He was too late. Rage filled Erik's mind. He looked at Tyrkir with hate in his eyes. Tyrkir, fearing Erik's rage, drew his axe back. Erik drove into him before Tyrkir could swing the axe at Erik. They sprawled on the gravelly beach. Erik grabbed

Tyrkir by the collar, lifted his head, and slammed him down with all his strength. Stunned, Tyrkir's world went black. Erik did not stop slamming Tyrkir into the hard beach gravel until Bjarni grabbed him by the shoulders and pulled him back. Only then did Erik look at Tyrkir and see his bloodied, misshapen head.

He staggered to his feet, wiped slobber from his mouth, looked at Bjarni, and said, "He had no right to murder Peluk, no right!"

"I can say that I saw Tyrkir raise his axe to attack you, but you got carried away with your love for that Skræling, Erik. You should think about that. He made a move that scared Tyrkir, and he thought he was acting in self-defense. With what experience we have with them; we are all on edge around them. We do not know if we can trust them. There will probably be many mistakes made resulting in death, but we Norse must stick together. We have very low numbers here and have no idea how many Skræling there are. For all we know, they may be watching us right now.

"I think you will have to pay Tyrkir's family a man bounty, though I never heard him speak of any family." He pointed to Peluk's body and said, "You take care of his body any way you like. We will take Tyrkir's body back to the ship. Gunnar, carry those hides to the ship. Olaf, help me with Tyrkir," Bjarni ordered.

Erik did not answer, he just looked at Bjarni with contempt in his eyes. *What does he know about any of this? Peluk saved my life. Bjarni has been in battle—he should know the kinship that forms when another man saves your life. Bjarni and the rest think since Peluk was a Skræling, he was not a real person. How wrong that thinking is. I think these people have feelings and a social order just like we do. Maybe I can convince Haakon of my feelings about the Skræling. I know that Peluk may have been able to help us in dealing with them. Now...?*

Erik picked up Peluk's body and slung him over his shoulder. *What should I do with you, my friend? You never did a thing to deserve your fate. Pe...my little friend went into that big house first. I almost forgot. I should not say his name, even to myself—evil spirits will come. Though, I do not see how things could get any worse for him. That must have been his home.* As Erik approached the tunnel entrance, he could see that Norsemen had entered and come out. *No telling what kind of mess they left behind.*

He struggled to drag Peluk's body through the tunnel and into the living area of the house. There was barely enough light filtering through the tunnel to make out some general shapes. He could not stand up straight. But after a few minutes his eyes adjusted, and he could make out a few items. The rock and earth walls were covered with animal skins that were old and worthless enough that the Norsemen left them untouched.

A hearth lay in the center of the room oriented with the entrance. On it lay a flat piece of slate and on that was a round soapstone bowl that was filled with solid animal fat. A fringe of burned fuzzy material was embedded around the rim. A pile of kindling material and some dried driftwood lay next to the hearth. Erik took out his flint and striker and quickly had a small fire going in the hearth. That gave him enough light to look around.

Now he could see that the Norsemen had pretty well ransacked the place. A few worn sleeping skins were scattered on the floor, but little else was to be seen. Along the wall opposite the entrance was a platform made of rocks large enough for a handful of people to lie on. Under parts of the platform were open holes where things were probably stored. Pieces of chert and other hard stones were now scattered about on the floor, most had sharpened edges. Here and there were small pieces of bones. A hollowed seal leg bone container lay on the floor with sharp pieces of bones, probably needles. The carved lid had been removed and cast aside. On one side of the platform were some small open spaces. Below them were balls of sinew thread of various thicknesses. Obviously, the Norsemen found no value in them.

On a couple of rock shelves embedded in the walls were small rock bowls filled with animal fat and that fuzzy material around the edges. It dawned on him that those must be lamps. He took a small flaming stick from the fire he had started and tried lighting the fuzzy material in one of those little bowls. It flickered fitfully for some time before finally lighting. The material around the rim slowly ignited until the whole rim was aflame, giving off a soft yellow glow that spread throughout the room.

Now Erik could see some of the trappings of these peoples' lives. There were ragged old cloaks hanging from pegs driven into the sod between the rocks in the walls. There were some soapstone pots, a few cups made from walrus skin. A couple of bags that may have been used to carry water hung from a peg near the platform. Everything looked worn out and abandoned. *Probably the better things were pilfered by my shipmates. Certainly, those skins Tyrkir had looked new and of high quality. I had better take care of my little friend and get out of here.*

Erik put the best skin he could find on the platform and laid Peluk on it, orienting him so that his head wound would not show. Next, he laid the boy's arms across his chest. The crippled arm was not long enough to make a good "X" in the center of his chest. He dug into Peluk's clothes until he found the seal amulet that hung around his neck. It was carved from driftwood but was well made. He arranged it so that it sat on his chest. Next, he reached into the decorated bag that Peluk carried and took out the seal/human mask, the little bag of yellow powder, and the small drum/drumstick set. He carefully set the mask on Peluk's face and sprinkled some of the powder on his chest. He put the drum and drumstick by the boy's side. Next, he took the talisman that Peluk had given him from his own shoulder bag and placed it in Peluk's good hand. Finally, he pulled out the raven and falcon wings and placed them on Peluk's chest. He had no idea if any Christian or Norse chants would help Peluk, so he remained quiet while doing these things.

About the time he was finished, Olaf's voice echoed through the tunnel. "Erik! Are you all right?"

Erik replied, "Yes, just finishing up. I will be right out."

Olaf yelled back, "The tide is coming in.

Haakon wants to get off this island and head back to West Greenland right now!"

"Rest in peace my friend, and may I find you in God's heaven one day," Erik said as he started to blow out the little lamps he had lit but then decided to leave them on. Other Skræling may see a glow and find a boy someone cared about.

CHAPTER 8

WEST GREENLAND

As he and Olaf climbed aboard the ship, Erik noted twelve rowers in place with oars ready to be shoved through the oar ports and put to work pulling the ship out to sea as soon as the water was deep enough to float them. Haakon was in his place in the back of the ship holding the steerboard.

When he saw they were on board, Haakon yelled, "Olaf, go below and help Gunnar and Sigi sort the Skræling things. When you are done, report to me what we have. Erik, come back here so that we may talk."

As Erik made his way past the rowers, he noted Bjarni scowling at him. Erik looked away.

"Tell me about this Skræling and what was so

special about him that drove you to murder a fellow Norseman." Haakon started the conversation.

"To begin with, that young man saved me from freezing to death," Erik replied defiantly. "Tyrkir had no right to murder Peluk. Every man on this ship knew that he was just a boy and crippled at that. He was absolutely harmless. Tyrkir knew that. He just killed him out of blind hatred for the Skræling. A hatred that is unfounded, I will add. I was hurrying to stop him but got there just too late. Tyrkir drew his axe back to strike me, so I plowed into him. The next thing I know, Bjarni is pulling me off Tyrkir. I never meant to kill him, I just wanted him to pay for murdering Peluk. I must have gone *berserk*.

"I know I will have to pay a man bounty to his family, I understand that. But he had no right to kill Peluk like that. Peluk could have, and I believe would have, helped us form a trade alliance with other clans of his people. Now that is all lost. Others will see that a clan village was looted and blame any Norsemen who come near their home-land. It is all so stupid."

"You are going in a lot of directions with your answer, Erik. Know this: Tyrkir had no family. He was apprenticing on this ship seven years past when his parents died of some unknown internal evil, a plague of some kind or food poisoning maybe. He was their only child and had no other relatives. So, there is no one for you to pay a man bounty to. Besides that, one could argue that he drew his axe back. Your claim of self-defense is justified. You need not worry about that.

"I, myself have done it and witnessed several times in battle that when a fellow warrior saves your life, you risk life and limb to protect him, cutting down any enemy that threatens him— even if that enemy is one of your shipmates. You will not be prosecuted, even if Bjarni is not happy about it; I have seen him do the same thing. As the man who killed Tyrkir, his body and possessions belong to you. Once we get in open water, I suggest a sea burial. You can do what you wish with his things." Haakon's manner was unemotional.

"Hoist the sail! Lookouts keep an eye on those ice blocks! We sail southeast to open water and back to West Greenland!" Haakon shouted to the crew. As soon as the sail snapped full, he shouted, "Rowers, ship oars!"

"Now, these other matters you spoke of, how will they know it was Norsemen who sacked their village? Who will tell them? Did you leave something behind?" Haakon looked seriously into Erik's eyes for the truth.

"Peluk was an apprentice to some sort of healer and spiritual leader of his clan. He seemed to know much about these things for one so young. He had seen but twelve winters, he told me. I believe that is how they mark their years—in winters. Anyway, he seemed quite skilled to me. He gave me a talisman he had carved from walrus ivory. It was a seal in a swimming posture. On the belly was a human/spirit face with blank eyes and the mouth forming a circle as if saying 'O.' All the features were very human except the ears stuck out oddly. I left that talisman on his chest because that is what he did with the old woman. The funeral ceremony he performed for her was quite elaborate." Erik spoke with a deep respect for Peluk.

"Wait, what old woman?" Haakon asked.

"When we first went ashore, and Peluk discovered no one had returned to the village, he climbed up a trail to higher ground so he could look out to sea. The tide was still going out, and less than four hundred paces to the north, he spotted a lump out on the mud flat. From up there I could see that this was only a small island, with a much bigger body of land just to the west. I had thought the village was on a peninsula, but it is really an island.

"When he saw the lump out on the mud flat, Peluk hurried as fast as he could to it. I followed. It was the body of a frail old woman, who it turned out, was Peluk's grandmother. She had drowned." Erik's face showed a sadness Haakon could not understand.

"Peluk communicated to me that all the others would have been carrying the heavy burdens of their possessions. She, being the eldest in the clan, would not have to carry anything. All the others would have been dragged to the bottom when the storm unexpectedly broke up the ice, most likely the storm we battled on the ship."

Erik gestured by waving his arm over the vessel. "He said this has been the warmest spring even the old woman could remember. The ice has never broken apart this early in the season. His people are very spiritual, and this early warmth has something to do with gods being offended, carrying their wrath to the people. Something about an old woman who lives under the sea feuding with the keeper of the ice or something like that. It was difficult to understand." Erik shook his head indicating he did not understand it all.

"At any rate, I carried her back to the village..." Erik's long explanation was wearing on Haakon's patience.

"Yes, yes, a fine funeral. Just get to the point where the other Skræling will know it was Norsemen who sacked their village," Haakon said impatiently.

"As I was saying, these people are very spiritual. They have great respect for the spirits that guide their lives and do all they can to not offend them. Kind of like our old pagan religion.

"Leaving those houses in disarray and stealing all the valuables is something they would never do, nor would any of their enemies. They would know it had to be some *strangers*, and the only foreigners they would know about would be, '*Strange, powerful men who come from the east in great canoes with giant wings attached that carry many men with hairy faces who wield terrible weapons.*' Word has gotten around—they know who we are.

"Another thing...the Skræling that killed our kinsmen in Markland and Vinland had used bows and arrows. I saw no bows or arrows among Peluk's people. They used only spears and harpoons for weapons. There must be different nations of Skræling we are dealing with. It could be that Peluk's people are not warriors at all," Erik said grimly.

"Well, if they retaliate, or attack us in any way, we will wield those terrible weapons, and they will know to fear us and do as we say," Haakon replied haughtily.

"With all due respect, Uncle, do you think they will trade their fine skins and ivory with us if we bully them? Would it not make more sense to befriend these people and trade honestly with them? There may be other clans around, and these Skræling can help us make friends among them all. Norway could become a powerful dealer in the exotic goods of this strange world. And you could become a leading merchant in that trade!" Erik's enthusiasm was building.

"We will not 'deal' with them if they try any trickery, for which they are known, I might add. Their language is impossible to learn. Just because you and this Peluk got along does not mean he has the heart of the others. As you said, he was a cripple and found out early, no doubt, in order for him to get along, he had to bow and scrape to everyone. His leaders could be of another ilk," Haakon said with finality in his voice, then added, "I will consider your words. Now I want you to go take Bjarni's place on his rowing bench. Tell him I wish to speak with him. It won't take long. Afterward, you had better get on with Tyrkir's funeral so the men can get some rest—in three days we should arrive in the western settlements."

"You wish to speak with me, Haakon?" Bjarni asked as he approached the rear of the ship.

"Yes. I wanted to talk to you further about this afternoon's actions out on that beach. Erik made some good points. What do you think our relationship is with the Skræling in these waters?" Haakon started the discussion with a question Bjarni had never expected.

"Why would I care?" he answered nonchalantly. "We come here, vastly superior in every way. We take what we want. They can either take what we want to give them or be killed. Simple as that."

"Bjarni, we have known each other a long time. What makes you think it is that 'simple?' These people have been surviving in these waters for a long time; do you think they are simpletons? When word gets around that we ransacked one of their villages, and everyone in it is dead, the rest will have nothing to do with us. There will be no trading. They know the territory far better than us—we will be ambushed at every turn and suffer great losses. Norsemen will have little success making allies of these people."

Bjarni cut him off. "They will soon learn the folly of resisting our people! Englishmen, with superior weapons and manpower, have had to surrender to our will. All of Europe trembles at the approach of our longships. And Europeans are much more prepared to fight than these dirty underlings...they're not even real men. How Erik could think that a Norseman's life was worth that of one of them is beyond me."

"Ah, you are yet young with a head full of grandeur. In truth, we have overpowered English and Irishmen only through surprise. These days they are more and more prepared for us, and we suffer too many losses in battle. Our wenches cannot fill our ranks as fast as we sacrifice them on battlefields. Did you know that this youth that Tyrkir killed was some kind of holy man or at least apprenticing to be one? Even with his family gone, his death will have wider impacts. Those people will not tolerate us wantonly killing their holy men."

Haakon's tone became somber as he went on. "I see only trouble coming for Greenlanders, and Tyrkir's blindness is but one example of a fool-hardy belief that we can overpower anyone we wish." Haakon's face had turned to stone.

"I told Erik he would not be punished because there is no family to repay. I told him to do with Tyrkir's belongings what he wishes. If you want any of his things, go speak to Erik about it. Don't take my actions as weakness—just practicality. Now go back to your bench so Erik can prepare

Tyrkir's body for a sea burial today." Haakon looked at Bjarni as he spoke in a serious tone.

"We will speak of these things again," Bjarni said with warning in his voice as he went forward to his rower's bench.

"Go prepare Tykir's body for burial. And bring me the medallion he has hanging around his neck. You can have anything else of his you want," Bjarni told Erik in an authoritative voice.

Erik looked at him and glanced at Haakon who was studying the afternoon sky.

Erik got up and started to go below deck where Tyrkir's belongings were laid out by his sleeping skins. "Is there anything special you want to say or for me to say about him before sending his body into the sea?"

"I will let you know later," Bjarni replied gruffly.

———

ERIK GATHERED Tyrkir's belongings and sleeping skins then went back on deck where his body lay under a wool blanket in the front of the ship.

After reporting to Haakon on what was taken from the Skræling village, Olaf joined Erik in preparing Tyrkir's body for burial. Erik laid out four ropes and placed the blanket over them. Next, they maneuvered the body onto the middle of the blanket. They respectfully removed Tyrkir's caribou skin outer tunic. Erik removed the silver chain with the eagle medallion and set it off to the side. Then they carefully put Tyrkir's steel chain mail on over his wool inner tunic. They left the caribou leggings and outer boots in place but took off his leather waist belt and retied it over the chain mail. Erik then folded the caribou hide tunic and laid it across the dead man's legs. Next, with some difficulty due to death stiffness setting in, they folded the arms over the dead man's chest. Erik removed the sword from its scabbard and laid it lengthwise on the center of the body and under the crossed hands. Olaf laid the man's bow and quiver at his side. Erik made sure Tyrkir's neck, waist, and ankle knives were all in their proper places. The rest of Tyrkir's few possessions were laid neatly on his legs. Finally, they placed his helmet over his already blackened face. Erik could feel the broken bones shifting as he struggled to get the helmet in place. It had a noseguard which helped cover some of the discolored face.

Having the body prepared, they folded the blanket over the head and feet first, then both sides neatly over the body so that it was completely covered. The ropes were tied off to make a bundle in the shape of a man's body.

Finally, they laid Tyrkir's shield over the body. While working, Erik and Olaf remained silent, but both were overwhelmed by the stench of death emanating from the body. When the violent death came, both his bladder and his bowels had emptied into his trousers, adding to the discomfort.

Having completed the preparation, they went below to the hold and found a loose plank, carried it to the deck and put the body on it. Erik quietly went around to the crew and asked five members to help Olaf with lifting the plank and sliding Tykir's body into the sea.

Erik felt awkward as he gave a eulogy and an awkward apology for the death of Tyrkir. Finding any praise for the man who murdered his friend was difficult. He felt great relief when Tyrkir's weighted body slid off the plank into the sea. Afterward he handed the medallion and chain to Bjarni, who placed a hand on Erik's shoulder and said, "Well done, Erik. This episode is now laid to rest."

———

THE PASSAGE across the Greenland Sea was fast and uneventful. The weather was fair, and a stiff westerly breeze propelled *The Sea Mare* smoothly to its destination. As the ship turned into the fjord leading to the Western Settlements two days later, the crew gave a loud cheer to Haakon for getting them there safely. He replied that they all shared in the task. A good share of the residents of West Greenland greeted them at the docks, with many volunteers eager to help them get unloaded and all their equipment, supplies, gear, and skins hauled up to Thorkell's Great Hall.

Everyone was in a festive mood for at first sight, it appeared to be a highly successful trip. By the time Erik and Olaf reached the Hall, Thorkell had heard the news of the loss of the best bear hunter he had ever known. He was not in such a festive mood when he laid eyes on Erik.

Thorkell called Erik to the center of the table and told him to give a detailed account of all that happened with the bear. When Erik was finished, Thorkell took a long drink of mead from his horn tankard, wiped his mouth on his sleeve, and told him he could have a seat at the great table—but down near the end, out of his sight.

Haakon and the rest of the ship's crew were seated closer to Thorkell. Olaf chose to sit with Erik. He told Erik that Thorkell was just upset at losing Lathan, that he would be friendlier in the days to come. After all, it was no small feat for Erik to kill that great bear, and Thorkell always admired such acts of strength and bravery.

Erik brooded over all that had happened, good and bad, as he drank himself into a depressed stupor. Olaf tried to cheer him up, but the more he thought of his own selfishness, the more depressed he became.

After Thorkell's banishment to the far end of the table, all the others left him alone. One of the maids serving mead tried to get him to talk to her, but he would have none of it. Eventually Olaf hauled him off to his sleeping room where he flopped down on a pallet and promptly fell asleep.

As the morning light filtered into the room from the smoke hole in the roof, Erik began to stir. His head felt like one of his father's great horses kicked him. About then, Olaf came stumbling in, smelling of the flowers the maid he'd been frolicking with used for perfume. Olaf laughed as he slurred, "While you were brooding over your slight from Thorkell, I was 'brooding' a fair maiden! You really take life too seriously."

Erik replied, "Maybe that is because I've seen it from a different angle than you. And must you talk so loud?" Olaf laughed and started to say something else but fell fast asleep before he got it out of his mouth.

Later that day, Thorkell summoned Erik to his

place at the center of the table in his Great Hall. Sitting in his ornately engraved High Chair, Erik's uncle exuded great power, making Erik feel small and worthless.

"I have talked to witnesses who watched you kill a Norse warrior because he killed a young Skræling. Sorting through all the words, I came to the conclusion that you acted with honor, retaliating for the death of a young boy who had saved your life. You need feel no shame for your actions.

"As to the bear incident, I can see that you did what you could. Circumstances guided your actions, and you tried all you knew to help Lathan. I am surprised that he let a bear get the better of him.

"You should not have ill feelings about what has happened. The transition from boyhood to manhood is filled with difficulties, and I feel you stood the test," Thorkell told Erik plainly.

"Thank you, Uncle. Your kind words mean much to me. I will strive to be a better man in the future," Erik replied.

"I pray your return voyage is quiet, and your future is prosperous. If my plans hold together, I will see you in Ulfrstadt in two summers. Give your father hale greetings from me. Go now, and enjoy your time in our fair land," Thorkell finished the conversation. Erik gave a slight bow and turned from the table. He wished Thorkell's words had made him feel better, but he still felt unworthy.

Over the following three days, Erik and Olaf toured Thorkell's vast holdings on horseback. They hunted caribou with bows and arrows and water-fowl with falcons. Both young men were quite skilled with weapons and were up and coming falconers. Evenings were spent drinking mead in boisterous revelry with the ship's crew and some of Thorkell's men. Erik even found himself in a maiden's bed one morning.

All in all, the Greenland trip was filled with mixed emotions for Erik. For him, the good things were overshadowed by the bad. He could not block the remorse he felt for the four deaths he felt responsible for. *Had I not let myself get separated from Lathan and Keir, they would both still be alive. If I had been quicker to see the problem, Peluk would not have been killed by Tyrkir, and I would not have killed Tyrkir. That is the truth no matter how you look at it,* Erik reminded himself every time his mind drifted to the tragedies, which was often.

———

FIVE DAYS after returning to Thorkell's farm in the Western Settlements, the ship was loaded and ready for the return voyage to Norway. They would stop in Brattahlid, the Eastern Greenland settlement, for two days to take on more bales of wool and seal skins. Then they would sail to Iceland where Haakon's second knorr lay waiting for them. Bjorn Ivarrsson commanded that ship. Among other things, he was in Iceland to recruit crew members and warriors for next spring's raid in Northumbria.

CHAPTER 9
RETURN TO NORWAY

Haakon's *Sea Mare* was loaded with bales of Greenland's finest wool, skins of caribou, polar bears, wolves, foxes, seals, and walruses. Bundles of narwhal and walrus tusks and whale teeth, a few crates of polar bear skulls, small barrels of polar bear teeth and claws, four large barrels of whale oil, and a small supply of green crystals and meteorite iron rounded out the cargo returning to Norway. The Greenland wool was recognized for its quality and would fetch high prices. More than enough to pay for the oak boards and few sheep they had hauled on the voyage to Greenland. Haakon would be happy with his share of the profits from this trip.

Haakon had lost only one man and was still saddened by the death of Thorkell's thrall, Lathan.

He was a good young man, possibly a nephew. Thorkell had come to think so, over the years following Sigurd's death. Haakon's brother believed he could see Sigurd in Lathan's eyes, even though they were of a different color, as he matured. Feeling remorse for not recognizing the man's heritage, Thorkell promised to care for Lathan's widow for the rest of her life.

———

I AM TRULY LOOKING FORWARD to getting back to Father's farm. I must make up for the way I left things and show the man I am ready to take on my role at his side, Erik mused.

Olaf will do the same, going Viking with Haakon. He can have it. As for me, I no longer want to be part of the Norse world that destroys everything they see and makes enemies in every port.

Erik decided, as he stood at the bow and looked at the empty sea in front of him, *I would rather build things than tear them down. A life where I can make things better instead of going to a foreign land, burning halls, killing defenseless people, and having a few pieces of silver and gold to show for it no longer appeals to me.*

I will also try to tell those I meet that the Skræling are not half-human savages, rather, they are highly skilled inhabitants of a wildland who happen to be different from Norsemen.

I am pleased that Thorkell informed Haakon that in two summers he would be coming to Norway to visit his brothers and conduct some business. Those family meetings have always been rousing and rowdy events. Maybe by then I will feel some joy and accomplishment.

They had set sail with the tide in mid-June and only stopped for two days at Brattahlid to trade news and take on a few fresh provisions for the voyage to Norway. They stayed only three days in Iceland and left there with a sister ship for the four-day voyage to Ulfrstadt, Norway.

Late afternoon on the third day out from Iceland, Olaf walked up to Erik, who was studying the view from the bow. They had a tailing west wind and were making good time as they crossed the ocean. Just as Olaf approached, Erik turned and yelled, "LAND!" toward the ship's crew and Haakon who, as usual, was at the steerboard. He turned and stared at the high clouds swirling around the highest peaks of Norway. The mountain tops slowly came into view. With the wind at their backs, they would make port by the next midday.

"Ah, the homeland is always a welcome sight!" Olaf exclaimed and slapped Erik on the shoulder.

"Yes, especially after this voyage," Erik replied glumly.

"Why are you so out of sorts? You should be the happiest man aboard this ship. What with killing the biggest bear anyone has ever seen and having a ship full of fine wool and exotic trade goods, even some of the exotic Skræling furs—it has been a great trip," Olaf said with too much enthusiasm.

"I see the blank stares of Lathan's and Kier's frozen faces and the little Skræling's disbelief that his head was split open, not to mention Tyrkir's misshapen head after I killed him with my bare hands," Erik replied sadly. He had not forgotten his friend's plea to not name the Skræling dead. "Had I been half a man, I could have prevented all four of those deaths. This trip turned into a nightmare for me."

"You are too hard on yourself. Bad things happen, you cannot prevent that. But you should celebrate the good things—they are just as important," Olaf answered. "Gods, in a fierce battle, you can lose forty of a hundred men. You just have to push onward, without looking back," Olaf continued.

"You always see things in a different light than I do." Erik still had sadness in his voice. "The boy was no older than Sven. I cannot imagine him doing the things that little Skræling could do. Sven will be all excited and want to hear every detail of our voyage. There are many things I do not wish to relive. How will I be fair to my brother?"

"Many people are going to want to hear your stories—that's why we go on these 'manhood' voyages—so we can brag about our exploits. Cheer up! The sun is setting on our backs, the mountains of home are before us, and we will be on land tomorrow. Right now, there is still some mead left. Let's go help finish it! Come on," Olaf pleaded gaily.

"Maybe it will help me sleep." Erik turned and followed Olaf below where the last mead barrel had just been opened. All the men not on oar or sail duty were ready to celebrate the final night at sea.

CHAPTER 10
HARALD'S SURPRISE

The sun was pushing past its peak into the western sky when Haakon told Bjarni to blow the conch shell ship's horn. The sails were being lowered on *The Sea Mare* and *The Sea Cow*, Haakon's two seagoing knorrs, as they eased up the fjord toward Ulfrstadt's wooden docks. The trumpet-like blast echoed up the fjord and throughout the deep valley, alerting the local residents of their arrival.

Twenty-four men used twelve oars to propel each ship toward the docks. Haakon, at the steerboard, gave orders to guide *The Sea Mare* into position. When the ship was where he wanted it and moving at the correct speed, he gave the order, "Ship oars!" In a coordinated, smooth motion, the oars slid back through six ports on each side of the ship and stowed in racks located just inside the gunwales on both sides of the deck. Hands hurled loop-ended ropes to waiting men on the dock. Haakon lowered the steerboard to the deck and tied it down. Doing so lifted the rudder up above the waterline strake and parallel to the length of the ship to keep the rudder from being damaged while the ship was at the dock in shallow water.

A crowd had gathered near the docks. Some would help unload cargo from the ships and load wagons to be taken to storehouses on Haakon's farm on the hill just east of Ulfrstadt. Others were there to greet the sailors, who had been gone for fourteen months. A few were vendors who hoped to sell food, trinkets, drink, or snuff to anyone interested. Still others gathered out of curiosity to hear news of wherever the ships had come from. Among the throngs were those who practiced the art of picking pockets and seeing what they could abscond with exerting little effort.

The weather was favorable, with a few high clouds, a light western breeze, and warm, midsummer temperatures. The hills and moun- tains were still covered with green grasses and forest, though the deciduous trees were beginning their transformation toward fall. The various green shades of the trees and grasses contrasted sharply with gray rock outcrops and cliffs in the higher elevations. Snow still capped the mountain peaks to the east.

Erik stepped off the ship with his big duffel slung over his shoulder. Two young Irish thralls from his father's farm came up and offered their help. He sat the big bag at their feet, and it took both to handle it. "Bradan, Caomh, you've both grown since last I saw you."

"Aye, your family feeds us well, Master Erik. And welcome home. Your pa will be arriving soon, my lord," Bradan said enthusiastically. The Irish thralls spoke in a mixed Norse-Irish pidgin.

"It is good to be on dry land," Erik replied. He spied his father coming down the worn path that led to the docks.

Jarl Harald Rolfcarlsson was dressed in a lightweight gray woolen tunic and light gray canvas trousers. Plain heavy leather boots covered his feet. He was still a large, powerful presence despite his graying blond hair and clean-shaven face.

"Erik, my son, you know not how good it is to see you and so healthy looking, too!" Harald proclaimed as he strode up to Erik and embraced him like a long-lost friend.

Erik was taken aback. "I expected a less exuberant welcome," was all Erik could think to say.

"Ah, well the past is the past, let it lay there. 'Tis time to move forward. We've much work to do and no time for bickering. There is a whole future to build; let's get on with it, my son," Harald said with a wide smile. He held Erik at arm's length, holding his shoulders and looking him up and down. "You've changed, son, grown up, matured. You look as though you are ready to fill a man's shoes. I will want to hear all that happened in time. But if there was great danger involved, do not tell your mother. There will be time enough to tell all your stories. I have another matter to discuss on our way back to the hall. Where is Haakon?"

"Just over there, still on the ship, taking care of matters there. I am sure he will want to direct the unloading of the cargo," Erik replied evenly.

"Father, I wish to offer my apologies for the way I left," Erik said solemnly, looking his father in the eye. *Odd. When I left, I still had to look up to Father's eyes, now we meet eye to eye.*

"There is no need for apologies, son. As I said, that is behind us. You were a boy then, now, you are a man."

"I learned much more on the trip than I ever expected to. Some things that you may find appalling. There were good things, but many things that cannot be forgotten that should not have happened." Erik looked at Harald with remorse in his eyes.

"Let me go greet Haakon, then we will go home, and you can tell me all of it." Harald put a hand on Erik's shoulder and gave him a reassuring nod.

Harald found his way over to Haakon. They gave each other a hearty brothers' embrace. They made promises to meet the next day to discuss the voyage and make any settlements necessary.

"Now, why has this trip made you so dour? Haakon tells me you have the biggest ice bear skin and head any man has ever seen. I would think you'd be beyond proud of that," Harald told Erik when he got back to where Erik waited.

"The bear hunt was a nightmare, Father. I will have terror-filled dreams the rest of my life because of that hunt."

"Why, if I might ask?"

"Because three dogs, three good men, and a strange boy are dead because of that bear and my foolishness. I only killed him out of some unexplained chance of luck. I do not even know how to tell the story except to say I wish I could forget the whole episode."

"Perhaps that story can wait."

"You said you had something to tell me on the way to the hall?" Erik asked.

"It is fairly significant. I am not sure you are ready to hear what I have to say." Harald studied Erik to judge his reaction.

"I am ready," Erik said stoically.

"All right. Near Bergen, there is a powerful stockman. I have done business with him since he relocated there a few years past. He has a daughter your age, and we have arranged your marriage on the Equinox. Her name is Erna. You will be making your household in my hall. Everything is arranged. The bride price is three broken horses, including a bred mare, and a milking cow," Harald said seriously.

"Rather sudden, I must say!" Erik exclaimed. "I know our customs, but I am stunned. I expected to have some time to settle my feelings about the Greenland trip before another big change took over my life."

"Grown men find few opportunities 'to let feelings settle,' son. You just move from one crisis to another, and deal with each one as it comes. Remember, at nineteen years old, I watched my own father die in far-off Greenland, then immediately had to assume my role as master of his estate and Jarldom. I had no choice, no time to 'settle' my feelings. You will be a husband and ready to be master of all this if something should happen to me." Harald's voice was firm and uncompromising as he swept his hand across the area west of Ulfrstadt, indicating his holdings.

"What is the name of my bride's father, then?" Erik asked, not able to come up with a more appropriate question as Harald's great hall came into view up the winding trail from the town.

"Hermad Arvesson. He has a holding, much like mine, located just to the east of Bergen. With our families united, we will have a strong hold on the best horses and cattle in all of Norway. Your future should be prosperous," Harald answered in an even tone.

"He is the one who brought the stallion, Wild One, that you traded for four bred cows. Five years past, as I recall," Erik replied. "He seems like an honorable man. He must have several suitors lined up for his daughter. How did I get to be the chosen one? I did not know I was even looking for a wife."

"Yes, Hermad is an honorable man." Harald paused, gathering his thoughts. "Nearly all the young men are eager to go off raiding and making famous names for themselves as mighty warriors. You are no warrior, though you are intelligent, a hard worker, and you are honorable. Hermad did not want his daughter to become a young widow. You were the obvious choice."

Erik was taken aback that his father said he

was no warrior. *He said it as though it was a compliment. I am not so sure.* "I am as good with the weapons of war as any my age. Why am I *no warrior*?" Erik asked sharply. "And how does he know that I am not eager to go raiding?"

"Better than most. Son, you are good at everything you do, but your heart is not that of a killer. You show remorse when you kill a stag or even a stock animal to put food on our table. Warriors give no thought to any life but their own. I am proud that you see beyond the glory."

"You told him this about me?"

"I have the interests of this farm first and foremost in my thoughts. I see the blending of our families as a step in securing a prosperous future."

"So, I am merely a chess piece." Erik said it as a statement, not a question.

"Son, we are all '*merely a chess piece*' on the great board called life. Now, we will retire to the great room, and you can tell us of your Greenland adventures," Harald proclaimed as they approached his hall.

Walking up the road to his father's hall, Erik glanced toward the shipworks down the slope, on the beach next to the fjord. There was a large knorr under construction on the stony beach. The big ship appeared nearly completed.

"The shipworks is busy, I see," said Erik.

"Yes, an order from another lord of Bergen. That town is younger than Ulfrstadt, yet is growing larger every day. They will soon pass us, I suspect. That knorr will be finished in a few days," Harald replied.

When they stepped through the door, Erik was greeted emotionally by his mother, Astrid. "You look so grown up!" she exclaimed with tears running down her cheeks as she embraced her oldest son. She looked to Harald and read that he had already told Erik about his future. "Sven will be in from his busy day soon, the evening meal is prepared, and we all want to hear of your adventures." She smiled as she looked at him through tear-filled eyes, turned, and went back to the kitchen hearth at the north end of the great hall.

Before, during, and after the evening meal, Erik recounted a watered-down version of his trip to the west. Sven hung on every word about the caribou hunting and the great ice bear and was curious about the huge iceberg, but showed little interest when Erik talked about Peluk, the Skræling boy Erik encountered on the ice after the bear kill.

Late in the night, Harald finally spoke up, "We have much to do before we sail for Bergen. It is time we get to bed. Every day between now and the Equinox will be hard work, we need our rest. We will learn more about Erik's trip as we go along."

CHAPTER II
ERIK TAKES A BRIDE

H and on the tiller, Erik stood at the steerboard in the right-rear of Haakon's *Sea Mare*. *Two years past I looked out at that open sea beyond the prow post of this same ship. I had no idea of the events that would unfold before me. But it was all excitement and wonder.*

This time, the new life I am entering is just as mysterious and frightful. Then, I was not ready to be a man. Now, I am still not the man I always dreamed I would be, but this voyage will result in my lifetime commitment to a woman I have never met. While I understand the custom of arranged marriage, I am in no way ready to assume the responsibilities of a husband and, eventually, a father. How could Father do this to me?

"How long will it take us to get to Bergen, Father?" Sven asked Harald while they stood on the deck near the front of *The Sea Mare* and watched the open ocean come into view between the small islands at the mouth of Ulfrfjord.

"We plan to spend one night in a small fjord, son. We should arrive at the dock of Hermad's farm by midafternoon tomorrow, just after we pass the new and burgeoning village of Bergen."

"I hope there will be someone my age there. I am too young for the adult ceremonies and too old to play with the children."

"Hermad Arvesson has a large family. I think there is a boy about your age, and maybe a nephew or two. But you will be part of the groom's party and attend all the groom's ceremonies."

"Even where the mead will be flowing?"

"The sons of Harald Rolfcarlsson are required to grow up fast."

———

ERIK NERVOUSLY, but skillfully, moved the tiller, guiding the rudder, taking orders from Bjarni, who was stationed at the prow post, advising Erik of the navigational obstacles in the waterway. As he maneuvered the big knorr into a small fjord north of Bergenfjord, he moved the ship into a place where it could be anchored and provided shelter from the open sea. Once the keel was grounded two men leaped from the side with tie ropes and secured the ship for the night.

The tide ran out shortly before the sun rose, but the ship smoothly used the current to carry them back to the ocean for the short sail to their destination just east of Bergen. Again, Erik found himself at the steerboard controlling the ship to his soon-to-be father-in-law's holdings.

———

ERNA SMILED GRACIOUSLY when she first looked at her betrothed. *No one told me he is so handsome. Being a son of a stockman, I expected a brutish lout. He has knowing eyes, and he carries himself like a warrior. I will give him a chance!*

"Very pleased to meet you as well, Astrid Haraldswife. I trust your voyage to Bergen was satisfactory," Alfdis Hermadswife said politely.

"Yes, the voyage was satisfactory, though I abhor traveling on the sea. The ship is smelly and so unsteady. Put me on solid ground and give me some pleasant flowers to whiff, and I am happy. You keep a beautiful hall." Astrid nodded as her eyes took in the great hall, then turned her attention to Erna's mother. Hermad's hall was much like Harald's, with a framework of great posts and beams. The main difference was that it was much newer. A long table ran from one end to the other of the great room. A pair of intricately carved High Chairs sat at the middle of the long table. The walls were decorated with tapestries and stag heads. Light was provided by torches attached to the support posts and sunlight filtering in through the smoke holes in the roofline.

"Our humble hall welcomes all of you," Alfdis replied, gesturing into the cavernous great room. "It is with regret that I must say that your thralls and a few others will need to stay in temporary housing. We simply do not have enough space in the main hall for everyone attending the festivities."

"Our family wishes to be no burden on you, Alfdis," Astrid said sincerely.

"Oh, your family is no burden. This union will benefit both our families in many ways. Now, let us get a good look at this young man," Alfdis smiled widely as she grasped Erik by both elbows and turned him to face her. She looked up at his youthful face and said, "You are a handsome one. Welcome to our family!"

Erna looked away, blushing, as did Erik. Astrid smiled.

Mother! Why must you be so forward at a time like

this? Erna cringed at what her mother would say next.

"In my family, people never waste time trying to be too polite, we speak what we think," Alfdis said, knowing she had stepped over an invisible line in her daughter's eyes.

Erik surprised Erna when he replied, "Make no apologies, woman, we are pleased to be here, and I look forward to a long, prosperous relationship with your family."

"Erik, I would like you to meet my daughter, Erna Hermadsdottir. She is a strong and competent young woman, with wide hips, capable of bearing many children," Alfdis said cheerfully to Erik.

Our first touch, Erna thought as she reached a hand toward Erik. He took her hand gently in his, pulled it up and gently kissed the middle knuckle.

"Pleased to meet you, Erik Haraldsson," she blushed, but said calmly, hoping he could not feel her knees trembling.

"As I am pleased to meet you, Erna Hermadsdottir. I must say I am nervous about this whole business. But your lovely face and generous smile have a great calming effect on me." Erik had no idea where those words came from. *She is not beautiful, nor is she ugly.*

I can feel my face turning red, and my hand is

sweating in his! Erna always considered herself rather plain.

"Kiss him, Erna!" a young boy exclaimed as he came near the crowd in the big room.

"Mind your manners, Borg!" flew out of Erna's mouth before she could restrain herself.

"Excuse me. I will take care of Erna's trouble-making little brother," Alfdis said as she grabbed the ten-year-old boy by the arm and marched him to an empty corner of the great hall.

———

"WE ARE HERE on this first day of the wedding week to settle the bride price and dowry," Bjorn Sweinsson, official law reader of *Hordaland*, said as he looked at the men at the big table in Hermad's great hall. Present were Hermad Arvesson, father of the bride; Jarl Harald Rolfcarlsson, father of the groom, Erik Haraldsson, the groom, Sigfinn Hermadsson, older brother of the bride, Ingvar Hermadsson, uncle of the bride, Haakon Rolfcarlsson, uncle of the groom, Olaf Haakonsson, cousin of the groom, and Sven Haraldsson, younger brother of the groom.

"These items were agreed upon the fifth day of September, In The Year of Our Lord 1005, one year just past, according to this rune scroll I have in front of me. Our purpose here is to determine that these terms are the ones agreed to by both families, and to ensure the terms have been met. Before we finish our deliberation, we will inspect both the stock and the silver to agree that the quantity and quality promised have been met. Our conclusions will determine if the wedding can proceed. The giving of these items will be part of the ceremony on Friday morning. Is everyone clear on our purpose here today?"

Nods around the table indicated everyone understood.

The law reader looked at the rune scroll closely. "It says here that the bride price is three broken horses, including one bred mare, and a milking cow. Is that price agreed on by all parties?"

Harald spoke up, "It is the price Hermad and his wife agreed to. My wife agreed to this price before I sailed to Bergan with the proposal last September. Haakon, Erik, and Olaf were on a voyage to Greenland at the time, so they were not involved in the negotiations."

"I discussed the price with all of the men and women of my family," Hermad spoke next.

"Are there any objections to the bride price?" Bjorn asked. No one responded. "Then, let us adjourn from this table and proceed to the pens where the livestock is held."

After agreeing that the stock was as promised, the men returned to the table in the great hall.

"The dowry listed here calls for 120 pounds of silver coins. Is that agreeable?" Bjorn asked.

Is it worth that much to pawn a daughter off on me? Erik wondered.

No objections were raised, but Sigfinn raised his eyebrows when the amount was announced. The six bags loaded with silver coins were brought to the table to be counted and inspected. No surprises were found.

"It is my duty to ask if you have enough mead for the wedding feast and for the bride and groom to stay intoxicated during the required thirty-day matrimony period," Bjorn asked impishly.

"We have plenty—you and Brother Michael can stay as long as you wish!" Hermad laughed.

"From the official standpoint of the Jarl of *Hordaland*, whom I represent, the wedding between Erik Haraldsson and Erna Hermadsdottir can proceed," Bjorn announced, scribbling his mark on a document and pushing back from the table. "You would be wise to keep guards watching this hoard of silver, Hermad Arvesson," Bjorn cautioned.

"Of course," Hermad answered.

The men went outside where people were gathered near where the ceremony would be held.

Food and drink were shared, and the law reader announced the wedding could go forth.

————

SATURDAY WAS the big day for the bride and groom and the most anticipated by the guests.

Before dawn, the adult female relatives of the bride and groom, and a couple of special friends of the bride gathered in a bathhouse large enough to hold a dozen people. Erna removed the gilded kransen from her arm and placed it in a special pine box where it would be saved for her own daughter one day. Thralls placed a large pot in the room partially filled with water infused with crushed linden flowers, birch blossoms, and fir needles. When all the women were stripped of their clothes, they began lightly slapping one another with wet birch twigs to help induce sweat while red-hot stones were added to the pot. The resulting steam filled the air with a rich, sweet aroma and caused the women to sweat profusely. Erna was scrubbed with lavender soap to purify her body. Her hair was also carefully washed with the fragrant mixture.

When the other women were satisfied that Erna had been adequately cleansed and purified, they led her outside to a deep, clear pool in the creek and unceremoniously tossed her in. She plunged into the ice-cold water and came out breathless. She clamored up the steps on the bank where the others waited with towels to dry and warm her frigid body. The process started Erna on her path from childhood to womanhood and married status.

Erik was sent to an old crypt. He was ordered to break in and come out of the darkness with his grandfather's sword. The act would start him on his journey to adulthood. His next event was one like Erna's cleansing ceremony. He was stripped and sweated before being scrubbed with pine scented soap. After plunging into a different pool, he was taken to a room where his body and hair would be rubbed with fragrant oil before being dressed for the ceremony.

In his case, he wore a plain blue, long-sleeved tunic over black wool pants and newly polished black leather boots. His clothes were plain, but he wore a black leather sword belt with a large silver buckle with a carved wolf's head. Around his neck, he wore a silver chain with a thin dagger hanging down his chest. He bore no tattoos or other facial markings. He did wear a black leather headband to hold his shoulder-length blond hair off his whiskered face.

Erna wore a plain ivory-colored, finely woven

wool long-sleeved dress with simple embroidering in the same fabric and color around the high waist and down the sleeves. The dress buttoned high on the neck. She wore one silver chain that dropped onto her chest and another that held a small dagger that hung at the base of her neck and down her chest. She had a dainty silver ring on her right index finger, and another on her left-hand small finger. Her footwear consisted of simple ivory-colored, soft leather shoes.

Erna's face had been dusted with white ash powder and a light amount of rouge added to her cheeks. Silver hoops hanging from small chains decorated her ears.

Her waist-length, sand-colored hair was curled into ringlets that cascaded down her back. Her head was adorned with an elaborate crown made from woven wheat stalks and lined with silver piping and knots. Small fresh-cut, ivory-colored flowers highlighted the band around her head while long silver encrusted wheat stalks streamed from the crown down the back of her head to below her shoulders. The crown was the one her mother had worn twenty-five years past.

"How do I look?" she asked her best friend and attendant, Verna.

"You look worthy to be a king's bride," Verna beamed.

"Mother, what do you think?" Erna turned to give a full view of herself to her mother.

"I am jealous that it is you in that dress and not me. You look beautiful!" Tears appeared in her light blue eyes.

"Is it time yet?" a nervous Erna asked.

Her mother pulled a drape back and looked out a small window. "Nearly. Most of the crowd is gathering near the arbor, though your groom is not there yet." After a short pause, "Ah, here they come now. The warrior, Olaf, leads, then Erik. Your cousin follows, and Erik's brother, Sven is last. We can move to the door now."

The day was spectacularly sunny with a wisp of a southern breeze. The hills were at their autumn best, with hues of golden brown, orange, yellow, and the green of the evergreens. It was a perfect day for the outdoor wedding ceremony.

Brother Michael, a young priest, would officiate most of the ceremony, even though he was uncomfortable with the pagan rituals the Norse still insisted on using in their weddings. He stood under the arch made of elaborately woven birch limbs and branches that was built for the occasion. Erik walked up and stood to the priest's left side. Once the groom and his three groomsmen were in place, everyone turned and looked to the entrance of the main hall.

Presently, the big oak door swung open, and Erna stepped out with her three attendants following, and her mother at her side. Once the bride and her attendants were in place, Alfdis and Hermad were in their places, Brother Michael called out, "The bride price and dowry have been agreed upon and have been presented to the respective parties."

Next, he announced the sword ceremony. He explained the importance of the sword ritual and stoically praised the Norse for upholding the time-honored tradition.

Erik drew his grandfather's sword from the scabbard, held it so the point touched the ground between his shoes, reached into a pouch attached to his sword belt with one finger, and produced a simple gold ring. He slipped the ring onto the tang on the sword's hilt, turned, and presented the sword to Erna. While doing so, he recited a short list of vows. Erna held the sword with the point down as her brother walked up to her. He was holding her grandfather's sword. He took Erik's sword as he handed hers to her. She then presented it to Erik, being careful not to lose the ring hanging precariously on the tang on the side of the hilt and reciting her sword vows.

Erik and Erna slowly turned to Brother Michael as he went into a long explanation of the importance of the ring ceremony as part of a Christian marriage ceremony. When finished, he took the rings from the swords, and Erik and Erna turned and handed the swords to their first attendants and turned back to the priest.

Brother Michael said the ring vows with Erik and Erna repeating after him. After the rings were exchanged and placed on the appropriate fingers, Brother Michael had the bride, and groom hold hands and recite prayers for protection, peace, health, and fertility to the Norse gods Odin, Thor, Freyr, and Freyja.

At the conclusion, he told Erna to stay put while he, Erik, and the male attendants walked over to a cleaned barn where the feast was to take place. Erik waited by the door as Erna walked up. When she arrived, he held her and carefully walked her into the open area inside the barn. The motion symbolized the maiden moving into marriage with the assistance of her new husband. Once inside, Erik drew his new sword and thrust it into the low ceiling boards of the barn. He drove the sword in nearly to the hilt, signifying a strong union with his bride. Erna was awed by his strength.

In the large open area was a table with one chair. Erna sat in the chair while a thrall brought over an elaborate horn drinking cup sitting on a stand. Erna took up the cup while another thrall brought out a container of the special *bride's mead*. She filled the drinking horn to nearly full. Erna then presented the cup to Erik, her new husband. Erik made the sign of *Mjolnir*, Thor's Hammer, over the cup, toasted Odin, and drank half of it down. He then handed the horn to Erna, who toasted Freyja before drinking the rest of the mead. The thrall immediately refilled it.

Erna was instructed to sit back down. Verna brought over a silver Thor's Hammer and placed it in Erna's lap. Verna explained that *Var* witnessed the exchange of vows and would watch over the feast. She said a prayer to Thor asking for his blessing and protection of Erna's children. She explained that the placement of Thor's Hammer between Erna's genitals and her womb would insure Thor's protection while her children were in the womb.

After another drink and refill, Hermad made the announcement that the food was ready and invited everyone to partake in the feast. The feast and accompanying revelry lasted well into the night.

Erna finally made the announcement that she was drunk, while staggering in a circle and sloshing her drink over anyone close by.

At that point, Olaf, Sigfinn, and Ingvar, three

male witnesses, along with Verna, Mundgerd, and Ingrith, three female witnesses, accompanied Erik and Erna to their bedroom.

The drunken, inexperienced youths were a comedy act as they clumsily undressed and fell into the *bride's bed* to consummate the marriage. Erik's ability to concentrate on the task before him was compromised by Olaf's constant chiding and offers to show him how to get things done.

When Erik finally released his seed into his new bride, she immediately passed out, as did four of the six witnesses. Olaf and Verna were on the floor on a blanket doing a better job at copulating than Erik and Erna.

At midnight, four days later, the wedding celebration was finally completed. Most of the guests went on their way to their homes near and far. By custom, Erik and Erna remained in a semi-drunken haze for the next three weeks to finish consummating their marriage. Haakon and Olaf volunteered to come back after the honeymoon period and take Erik and Erna back to Ulfrstadt where they would begin their life as husband and wife.

Haakon's *Sea Mare* carried them from Hermad's farm to the open ocean where they sailed along the coast in fair weather. The day was sunny, and it was unusually warm for late October.

Haakon brought his big ship to transport the many wedding gifts the couple received. He also needed room to bring Erna's beloved blond colored mare, *Sifjar Haddr*.

Erik and Erna lounged on the deck on a blanket. Erna had fallen asleep. He studied her supine form with a smile on his lips. *How did I get so lucky? I expected a plain brute of a woman who had farming skills and little else. Now, I find myself being amazed constantly by her wit and knowledge. Her good looks and "better-than-most" body are a bonus. Once we got the lovemaking down, we can't stay away from each other. No wonder she fell asleep in this warm sun— she's had little sleep for a month now.*

I really expected a wife arranged by my father to be something to dread. Instead, I find myself falling deeper in love every day. More and more I find myself looking forward to a long life with this woman!

Together, they shared stories of their upbringing. Erik spoke respectfully about Peluk and how he had learned much from the boy about how his own countrymen treat unknown people and places. The more he talked, the more Erna seemed to admire him. He appreciated that.

CHAPTER 12
HOT POOL

They were nearing Ulfrfjord on the second day. Again, Erik and Erna were on a wool blanket on the deck enjoying another unseasonably warm day. Erik wore a light-weight gray tunic and thin, black trousers. His wide leather belt had no accoutrements hanging from it. Erna wore a light-weight blue dress that covered her knees and buttoned to her neck.

Erik decided they needed more time together and developed a plan to take her up into the highlands on the farm where there was a pool of hot water that bubbled up from deep in the earth. His ancestors had developed a small campground by it. The spring was far enough away from Harald's Hall that they could enjoy their privacy.

After arriving at the docks by Ulfrstadt at

midday, the rest of the day was spent moving wedding presents and gear from Haakon's knorr to Jarl Harald's Hall. Erik took the time to get Erna's prized mare settled into her new surroundings and introduced to her stablemates.

Erik was shocked when Harald offered no resistance to his plan to take his new bride into the hinterlands to spend time together.

"Just be sure she is carrying my grandson before you return to the farm," Harald chided Erik with a smirk.

"I will do everything in my power," Erik replied with a wink.

Erik and Erna spent a half day packing food, clothing, bedrolls, tarps, fishing gear, and a tent. Sven warned Erik that he had seen bear tracks near the big pond on the trail to the hot spring. Erik loaded his spear, bow, and quiver as a precaution, but doubted they would be needed.

As the sun rose the next morning, Erik and Erna left the fenced horse pens. The unseasonably mild weather continued. He was on his black gelding with a white star on its forehead, Erna on her blond mare, and a brown packhorse with white stockings on three legs carried their gear. Almost as soon as they left the pens, the trail began to climb.

They followed the established trail up through

sparsely wooded pasture land as they gained nearly a thousand feet of altitude before they reached a high meadow of rich grasses. Erik stopped to give the horses a rest. The couple dismounted, and Erik allowed the horses to wander south a short distance to drink from a babbling stream that cut across the meadow.

From where they stood, Erik turned back to the north and pointed the spectacular view out to Erna.

"Oh, Erik, it's beautiful!" Erna exclaimed.

"I have always loved this place," Erik replied as he looked out over the valley. Much of the fjord was visible, Harald's Hall was quite clear, as was the village of Ulfrstadt with its trading bazaar and cluttered rim of houses. Gardens of harvested cabbage and other vegetables were scattered around the village, then larger fields of barley and self-sown wheat spread to the south and east. To the east, across the Ulfr River were extensive peat bogs. Erik explained that the peat was harvested and roasted for the iron contained in the plants.

"Yes, I know the process," Erna said.

Just east of the village, on a prominent hill, stood Haakon's Hall. It was not as impressive as Harald's, but it was much newer. Continuing the view up the fjord, the land became steeper as it rose to the high mountains. The fjord wound around the hills and disappeared from sight.

The north side of the fjord was just as spectacular with forests, meadows, and outcrops of gray rock. The land was steeper, with no dwellings visible. The hand of man was only represented by a few flocks of sheep still grazing the highlands.

After the visual tour of the valley, Erik led Erna across the meadow to the stream where the horses had had their fill of the frigid water. After remounting, Erik led the way to a ford before the trail entered a forest of spruce, pine, maple, and oak trees. An hour later, they came to a clearing, turned east, and started climbing again.

The trail followed many switchbacks as they climbed several hundred more feet in elevation. When they stopped to rest, Erna wanted a warmer wrap, as she noted the rapidly dropping temperature at the higher elevation.

Once fitted with a warmer tunic and a wool hat, Erna was ready to continue. The horses appreciated the break and once the items were removed from the packs, they found the nearby stream and satisfied their thirst. Erik and Erna enjoyed a piece of dried beef and some sweetbread. They refilled their canteens and readied for the last leg of their journey. The sun was well past halfway on its journey to the west.

Once back on her horse, Erna noted the trail turned to the south and leveled out. Maybe a half a league ahead, on the west side of the trail was a small lake. As they drew near, it was obvious fish were rising, creating small, widening circles of rippling water in random places across the surface.

"Will you fish here?" Erna asked.

"If we get to the campsite and get set up in time, I hope to catch our dinner," Erik replied.

Erna looked to the southeast and noted a column of steam rising from what appeared to be a small glen.

"Well let's get moving. I'm getting hungry!" Erna chided.

"You're the lord, my queen," Erik responded, and nudged his horse forward.

They reached the campsite with two hours of daylight left. The newlyweds went right to work setting up the tent, an outdoor kitchen of sorts, and the other necessities of comfortable camp life.

Once the horses were tended and the camp secure, Erik grabbed his fishing gear and led Erna back across the meadow to the small lake. In twenty minutes, he had two nice trout for their evening meal. Back at the camp he cleaned the fish while she got a cooking fire going. Erna prepared a dish of spinach and radish greens, sliced radishes, and beets along with a pan of hot grease for Erik's trout.

After their delicious dinner, Erik made the mistake of kissing his bride. One thing led to another, and before they knew it, they were in the hot pool, naked and exploring each other's bodies. Erik whispered what Harald had said about not coming back until she was carrying his grandson.

"I cannot promise a grandson, but I can say that I am carrying his grandchild," Erna replied proudly.

"Already? How can you know?" Erik questioned in disbelief.

"A girl knows," she said flatly.

Then she reached down, making sure his manhood was ready, and guided him into her while they were submerged in the hot water up to their necks. Their action was a bit slower than normal because the hot water kept washing away their natural lubricants, but they finally managed a tumultuous climax that took their breaths away.

Afterward, they crawled into the tent and continued making passionate love for another hour. When finished, they both collapsed into an exhausted sleep.

———

A FEW LEAGUES to the east and upslope a few hundred more feet, a large bear sniffed the westerly breeze. In the symphony of scents that he picked up, there was burned wood, horse, fish, and human. Ignoring the burned wood was easy because it was mixed with greens and roots. He had tasted fish and human before. He knew horses were big, powerful animals. They were also loaded with meat, no different from stags or elk. He liked meat. Humans could be trouble, but they filled his need for calories. And fish are always good. He started following the scents to their sources, drooling as he went.

Erik was sound asleep when he heard the horses nervously nickering. He sprung out of bed, took up his bow, and strung it. Then he slipped his quiver over his bare shoulder and stepped out into the predawn of early morning. Looking at the camp, he was disgusted with himself. They had gotten so carried away with their lovemaking, they had completely ignored cleaning up. Their clothes were scattered from the small table where they had eaten to the hot pool. More importantly, there was food half eaten on their plates, and more in the pans. A whole loaf of sweetbread was untouched by humans but was crawling with late-season ants and beetles.

Erik was just about to go back to get dressed and start cleanup operations when Erna stuck her head out and asked him what was wrong. He started to say the horses were acting nervous when a bear growl broke the quiet of the early morning. That got the horses started with panicked screaming.

Eyes drawn to the sound, Erik saw the dark shadow in the dim light about thirty paces to the east. The horses were rearing, stomping, and trying everything to break their tethers loose. Erik had to do something fast.

"What is it?" Erna asked, in a panicky voice, as she stuck just her head farther out of the tent flap.

"Quiet!" Erik hissed while searching the shadows for the bear. His strung bow with a nocked arrow was in his hands and ready to draw as soon as he acquired his target.

Erna caught movement and noted an open mouth with large sharp teeth in the shadows about thirty paces to the east. Her primal fear would not let her hold back a blood-curdling scream.

Erik bristled but tried to whisper, "Get back in the tent, and be quiet!" It was louder than he wished. Erna recoiled and began to cry hysterically. Erik tried to maintain his concentration and eyes on the shadows where he thought the bear was lurking.

Suddenly, out of the darkness, the bear charged straight at Erik. He responded with a shouted command for the bear to "Back Off!" as he pulled the bow up to the ready position while drawing the string back to the shooting position.

In a snarling huff, the bear slid to a stop and stood up on his hind legs, making him a head taller than Erik. The bear twisted its powerful head and roared while spreading his forelegs wide in a very threatening posture. The bear was only about three paces from Erik.

Erik aimed his arrow for the center of the bear's neck and loosed his arrow. The razor-sharp iron point barely slowed as it sliced through the bear's thick neck skin, sliced through the trachea, continued through the esophagus, muscle, and connective tissue before wedging between two vertebrae, severing the bear's spinal cord. The bear dropped instantly just short of Erik's bare feet.

The bear's fall splintered the arrow's heavy shaft while the stub, with the point, was driven through the vertebrae and nearly protruded from the skin on the back of the bear's neck. The big predator lay there and quivered for several heartbeats.

Instinctively, Erik reached into his quiver for another arrow, nocked it, and pulled the bow up into the ready position. Only then did he realize another shot was not needed. Shaken, he let out a loud exhale and began to tremble all over. Visions of the Ice Pack on the Greenland Sea and another large bear entered his disorganized brain.

Erna's whimpering entered his conscience, and he hurried into the tent. She stood on the sleeping pallet wrapped in a thick wool blanket, shivering. He cast his bow and quiver aside and wrapped his big arms around her. Her 'hurt feelings' emotion quickly faded, and she pressed her face into his bare chest.

When Erna came to her senses, she opened her eyes and looked at Erik. Still wrapped in the blanket, Erna exclaimed, "You are stark naked!" She paused and added, "My hero. I'm sorry I screamed. I saw that big mouth and knew we were going to die and just could not stop myself."

"I must confess, that I peed myself," she said meekly.

He pulled her tighter to his body. "When I think about it, I think the bear was confused, and your scream scared him into action. Had you not reacted the way you did, he might be still out there threatening us. Your scream probably saved us," Erik said calmly.

Erik realized he was naked, cold, and standing on a urine-soaked blanket. "I think we should pack up and get back to the farm," Erik stated.

"Under the circumstances, I could not agree more," Erna replied.

"Why don't you slip into the hot pool and take a bath while I skin and harvest some bear meat. Then we can pack up and go," Erik suggested.

"I will modify that and fix us a quick breakfast while you bathe after getting all bloody butchering that bear," she replied.

"Done!" he exclaimed while pulling on his trousers over his underwear and wool socks.

Erik went out and settled down the horses before he started the difficult task of gutting and skinning the huge bear. He did a hurried job, and within an hour he had over thirty stone of red meat rolled up in the bear's skin. He then used the human urine-smelling blanket as a tarp to wrap the bundled skin and meat package. He hoped Erna's urine smell would help hide the offensive odor of bear from the pack horse. He knew it was an irrational thought.

After finishing with the bear, Erik went into the hot pool, clothes and all, to wash away as much of the blood as possible. When he got out, he hurriedly dressed in clean clothes and started breaking the camp. In less than an hour, they had everything on the horses and were ready to start back to Harald's Hall, about six hours away. They would make it by mid to late afternoon because most of the trip was downhill.

When they passed the small thicket, they were met by a whole new problem. Barreling out of the northwest was a thick wall of dark clouds. A brisk southeast wind was picking up. "Those clouds are bringing the first snow of the season," Erik said casually.

"Yes, and it looks like it is a bad one at that," Erna replied, looking seriously at the billowing clouds.

"Let us put on our heavy coats and rain slickers now so we'll be ready for it."

By the time they crossed the trout stream at the edge of the high meadow, the first pings of sleet began to pelt their faces. Before they reached the sloping pasture, Erna had her colorful wool scarf wrapped around her face with just her eyes and nose visible.

When they were less than halfway down the sparsely wooded pasture, the snow was falling in earnest. The snow began to accumulate rapidly, causing multiple problems for the couple as they descended from the heights.

First, the ground, after several days of above

normal temperatures, was relatively warm. The falling snow melted on contact, soaking into the soil. But as snow accumulated, the wet ground froze, making the surface under the snow layer very slippery for the horses to maintain their footing. That condition caused them to move slower which allowed the falling snow to pile up as they went.

The next issue was visibility. The snow was falling so fast, coupled with strong winds, blizzard conditions were quickly upon them. Erik, his horse, and the packhorse had made the trek many times and had a reasonable idea where they were and how to get where they wanted to go. However, Erna and her horse were quickly disoriented. It got bad enough very quickly that Erik had to string a line between his horse and Erna's. That arrangement slowed them down even more.

The result of those issues was that the trail soon completely disappeared. The trail had been established using natural features of the pasture. With those being obliterated by the accumulating snow and fierce winds, it became impossible even for Erik to follow the trail.

In the meantime, falling temperatures made it extremely dangerous to stop and try to shelter in place. They had to complete their journey to the safety of the farm. Erik led them slowly down the hill, then made his own switchbacks when he felt the slope becoming too steep and slippery. It was all guesswork. If they descended too far, they would enter bogland that they would become entrapped in. If they pushed too far north before turning back south, they would encounter a slope too steep to negotiate. Being all tied together, if one horse went down, they all would.

On more than one occasion, Erik led them straight into the heavily laden branches of one of the few large pine trees in the pasture. With no competition close by, the limbs and branches of the big trees went all the way to the ground. The resulting confusion of tangled branches, ropes, and horses used up more precious time and energy.

Erik began to get concerned when he noted the failing light. He knew they would never last the night away from his father's farm. He plugged on as best he could, but darkness was descending rapidly. Making matters worse, the howling wind made it impossible to check on Erna's condition. Even bundled as they were, she must be freezing.

Just when Erik was thinking they should seek the semi-shelter of one of the big pines, Erik's horse ran into a fence rail. They had made it to the horse pens! From there, he only needed to follow the fence to the gate and cross the pen to the big stone barn.

Erik had to dismount and push snow out of the way to open the gate. It took him an hour to get his three animals from the pasture, through the gate, across the yard, and through the doors into the barn. The total distance traveled was less than thirty paces.

Once in the barn, two stable hands rushed to help. Poor Erna was partially frozen to her saddle and had to stand near the other horses in the barn long enough for her wool pants to be separated from the leather and wood saddle. Erik was worried she would have frost-bitten fingers, toes, and nose. At first, he could not even see her blue eyes through the crusted snow on her eyelashes.

Erna was not able to speak for several minutes after they reached the warm interior of the barn. It felt as if her lungs were full of ice, the slightest intake of air causing severe chest pain. Gradually she began to take deeper breaths, but the stench of the livestock in the barn was nearly as bad as the freezing air outside.

Eventually, she was able to take a few steps and not stumble. Erik was at her side for support, but she was not sure if she wanted it. He had taken her to a remote camp, then a bear tried to eat them, now this storm nearly killed her. *Is this what living with Erik will be like—one catastrophe after another?*

Erik gently turned her to face him, undid her coat and his own, and pressed his warm body against her. She felt his warmth immediately and let him pull her into him.

"I-I-I g-gu-gu-guess t-there w-was n-no w-way y-you kn-knew the b-bear or t-the s-s-st-storm w-were c-c-coming, d-did y-you?" Erna stuttered.

"No. No idea about the storm until we saw it together this morning. But Sven did warn me that he had seen bear tracks up by the lake when he was fishing last week. I just thought Sven was being Sven, or if there was a bear, he would never bother us with a fire going and two of us in camp. But I did bring my bow, just in case," Erik answered.

"H-how d-do we g-get to t-the h-hall?" she asked.

"Only one way," he replied.

"Erik, what shall we do with this bear skin and meat?" a stable hand asked.

"Put it in a cold room for tonight. We'll deal with it when the storm passes," Erik answered.

He turned to Erna. "You ready to brave a hundred paces of storm for a warm room, a hot meal, and a hot bath?"

"And cleaner air?"

"And cleaner air." He laughed.

They wrapped themselves in their heavy cloaks again, walked to the door closest to the hall, and fought their way back out into the blizzard. Erna clung to Erik's arm all the way to Harald's Great Hall. The storm had not let up, and it was no easy task trudging against the hard wind and deep drifts. Erik led Erna to the side entrance of the kitchen that had some shelter from the elements, and they were able to enter without moving too much snow from the door.

They stomped into the kitchen storage area, knocking new snow from their clothes and boots. Moving into the kitchen area of the great room, they were met with open-mouthed stares from Harald, Sven, and Astrid.

Astrid was first to speak. "We thought we would find your frozen bodies on that mountainside. How did you get here?"

"Our story is a long one, Mother. Is there any food left from the evening meal?" Erik asked, anxiously.

"There is always food in this Hall," Astrid replied with a smile. She got up and walked to the storage box near the massive stone hearth. Reaching up to a shelf, she pulled down two wooden plates, then grabbed two forks and spoons. From the steaming box, she took out two large beef ribs with meat clinging to them. She placed them on the two plates, then reached a pot hidden within the fireplace and scooped out cooked carrots and turnips. Next, she produced a loaf of bread, ripped it in two, putting a big piece on each plate.

"Marna, pour these people a horn of mead," Astrid ordered her maidservant.

The refugees from the storm tore into their food like they had had no nourishment for a month.

"I'll have your story now," Harald declared.

Erik and Erna told the story, leaving out no details except the athletic lovemaking that took place on the mountain.

"Am I to understand that you disregarded my orders and did not stay on the mountain until you were certain you had planted my grandson in your wife's womb?" Harald demanded; his eyes boring into Erik's.

Sven's face displayed a snide grin as he also looked at Erik's squirming countenance.

"I can answer that question, my lord," Erna piped up. Her stuttering was gone. "Along with the more immediate events that took place on the mountain, I did manage to make the announcement to Erik that yes, I am with child. I cannot promise a son or daughter at this time, but I am pregnant."

"Well then, pour me another horn of that mead!" Harald called to Marna.

Erik looked at Erna with wonder in his eyes and a wide smile on his face. *Just over a month past I was worried sick that I was not man enough to be married. Now, I will be a father in less than a year! Life comes at you fast.*

"Back up on the mountain, Erik, it was Erna's scream that saved you from being mauled by that bear?" Astrid asked, raising her eyebrows.

"That is the truth, Mother. And I am eternally grateful," Erik replied.

"Then I expect you will never demand that she be quiet again," Astrid said with a smile and a wink to Erna.

"Yes, Mother," Erik said meekly.

Changing the subject, Harald added, "And the bear's arrival and demise led to your decision to come back early. I almost think the Almighty was guiding your actions. His hand surely showed your horses the path through the storm. I trust your prayers will shower praise on the Lord for bringing you back safely."

"They will be added to the ones already spoken, Father, and we will praise him abundantly for the life growing in Erna's womb."

Harald nodded solemnly.

"Did you save the bear's head? Can I see the bear skin tomorrow?" Sven asked excitedly.

"Provided the storm lets us. Now, everyone will move to their sleeping rooms. It is late, and we are all tired," Harald declared.

CHAPTER 13
TOR IS BORN

Erna could not escape feeling all alone going into the final stages of her pregnancy. All her life, her mother and two aunts had been there to heal and comfort her through every illness, injury, and calamity that befell her. Now, she was about to enter the most dangerous time a young woman would likely experience while her most trusted support team was a two-day voyage away. Just the anxiety of the nearing birth was bad enough, but not having her mother there to console her made her extra fearful. The fact that her baby was active in the extreme did nothing to calm her frayed nerves.

Astrid and Lokilla, Haakon's wife, did everything they could to calm Erna's fragile nervous system, but she remained edgy. Erik's inexperienced attempts at soothing Erna usually served to make things worse. Every little muscle twinge made her fear the worst.

The recently acquired house thrall, Cinnia, who said she had seen fifteen winters, told Erna she had been there for several births in her old home. "Me mother was a midwife, all the time helpin' with child births. I watched 'til I was old enough to carry water and such. I seen about all of it, I reckon. A few died, sure enough, but Mother was good, most of her new mums lived to bear more wee ones. I miss her more than words can tell," Cinnia confided in Erna, when they were alone.

"Would you be there to help me when it is my time?" Erna asked sincerely.

"Being as how I be here, and nowhere else in the world, I expect I will be at your side when the time comes, Mistress Erna."

"Thank you, you have no idea how much it means to me to have a younger person in the room with me. Sure, Astrid has been nice, as has Lokilla. But they seem so much older, and the midwife Astrid is bringing in is even older. Lokilla, being a shieldmaiden is even scarier," Erna whined.

"Now Erna, 'tis a good thought to have experience in the room. I seen my share o' birthin', but they seen more and will be knowin' what to do. Ye need ta relax and trust these folks. Astrid seems to have taken mighty kindly to ye, she'll be doin' her best to make sure you're around ta make yer family grow," Cinnia scolded Erna.

"You are right, of course. I am being foolish," Erna sniffled.

"Naw, yer just bein' a first time mum. All are nervous and scared, right up 'til the babe is suckin' on their teat, then they're happy as larks. You'll be the same, mark me words, mistress."

"I feel better already, Cinnia. Thank you for putting up with me."

"I be the thankful one for getting sold to folks who are kind to their slaves," Cinnia replied honestly.

"It saddens me that Haakon and his men took you from your home, and nobody 'bought' you. Haakon gave you to Hara'd's house as a gift."

"Be not sad for me, mistress, my people have had slaves and been taken as slaves since the sun first smiled on Ireland. 'Tis all part 'n parcel to a grand cycle, I think. Anyway, I was never forced, and I ain't been whipped since I got off that ship. I thank the Maker for that."

"You will never be forced or whipped in this Hall. You can count on that. My hopes are that you will be a freed person one day, with a family of your own."

"Let's not be daydreamin', now, Mistress Erna. Things are what they are, leave it that," the young thrall said with finality, and left the room.

———

"Not time to push yet, young woman. You need to let your womb open first. I can put but two fingers against the head. You have many more pains left before you need to push," Grimma, the old midwife, told Erna.

"But I have had these pains since dawn!" Erna exclaimed as she caught her breath between contractions.

Astrid wiped the sweat from her brow with a cool cloth, saying, "No one can hurry a baby, Erna. They all come when they decide. Your husband had me in pains for two full days and nights. I was completely exhausted when he finally made an appearance. Yet I was happy to bring him to my breast, even though I had not eaten in all that time."

"You're doin' fine, Mistress Erna, I seen much longer labors than yours," Cinnia said while holding Erna's left hand.

———

"WHAT'S WRONG, why is it taking so long?" Erik questioned rhetorically as he paced back and forth behind the long table in Harald's Great Hall.

"You should busy yourself with cutting firewood, or something useful instead of wearing a path in my floor," Harald replied.

"Producing your first grandchild is not useful?"

"You've done your part in it, son. Now it is the woman's time to produce. Babies are all different. Some come fast, some slow, some very slow, like you. Always the man waits impatiently when he could be doing so many practical things."

"Yes, let's go fishing!" thirteen-year-old Sven spoke up.

"Good idea, Sven, the salmon should be starting their run. Let's get our rods and flies and have at them. Darkness is coming, and they'll be biting," Harald said happily.

"You go, I'm staying right here," Erik said emphatically, though he yearned to be standing on the creekbank casting flies into clear pools below big rocks in the turbulent river.

His father and brother were only gone a short time when Cinnia came down the hall to announce, "The baby has crowned!"

"What does that mean?" Erik questioned anxiously, all alone after Harald and Sven had left. He jumped up and stood on trembling legs.

"It means the womb is opened, and the babe's head is ready to come out! Twill be time for Erna to push shortly," Cinnia shook her head at Erik's ignorance as she wheeled and went back to the room where Erna was giving birth.

Erna pushed with all her might and felt herself open up when what seemed like a great oak log squeezed from her through her birth canal. She saw Grimma lift the child up by its feet and give its butt a swift smack. The child gasped and started to wail. The old midwife placed the baby in Astrid's hands, took out a heavy sinew cord and tied off the umbilical cord in two places close to the baby's tummy. Next, she unsheathed her razor-sharp waist knife and quickly sliced the cord close to where she had tied it off. Moments later, Erna, with one last contraction, expelled the afterbirth. Then, everyone in the room breathed a sigh of relief. Mother and child came through the birthing process healthy and strong.

As soon as Grimma and Astrid had the child clean, they handed the screaming boy to Erna. He hungrily took her nipple and contentedly suckled until he fell asleep. Tears of joy rolled down Erna's cheeks.

When everything quieted down, Cinnia went out to tell Erik he had a healthy baby boy. He grasped the young woman, lifted her off the floor and danced in a circle.

"Gracious be, Master Erik, I don't know if this is proper!" she called out.

"Proper or not, it's a joyous moment, dancing is in order!" Erik exclaimed, then what he was doing sunk in. He put the thrall back on her feet and looked at the floor. "Sorry," he said quietly.

"I think the Lord'll forgive ye this one time," she replied, straightening out her dress and apron.

CHAPTER 14
HARALD ROLFCARLSSON

"Father! Father!" Tor screamed at the top of his seven-year-old lungs. "Papa is hurt, he is not moving!" He was running as fast as his legs would carry him down the hill from the horse barn and pens to the beach where the shipworks was located.

Erik dropped the adze he was using to shape a deck board for the big knorr he was working on. "What? What is it? What happened?" Erik quickly noted his son had tears in his eyes. This was serious.

"The horse, Bold One, kicked him. He fell in the mud and was not moving or talking. I tried to wake him, but he did not move. Bradan and Caomh are with him." Tor burst out through his sobbing. He was worried that his grandfather was damaged beyond help. He could not imagine life without his papa.

Erik's mind was a whirl as he ran up the hill, leaving Tor in his tracks. *God in Heaven, please let him be all right. He is so important to the family, please let him survive. Tor idolizes him, and Father is so proud of Tor and his abilities. Tor makes him smile, but Gerna is the light of his eye. At only two years, she is just learning her way in the world. She makes him laugh. Until she started talking, he had not laughed since Mother died, five years past. Tor had many funny things to say when he was two and three as well, but Father was in no mood for laughter in those dark days after Mother's death.*

As Erik topped the hill and the horse pens came into view, he could see the two Irish stablemen tending to him. They had been part of Harald's farm for years, practically part of the family. Taken on a raid by Haakon and given to Harald when they were in their early teens, they were now fully integrated into the Norse way of life. Both were good with horses and hard workers —something Harald appreciated. They were now freed men working for wages.

"How is he?" Erik called as he scaled the fence and jumped into the breaking pen, barely slowing his approach.

"His heart is beating pretty fast, and his

breathing is steady but shallow. He has not opened an eye or said anything. I am pretty worried, looking at that bruise on his head," Bradan said in a worried voice.

The impact site where the horse hoof contacted Harald's head was clearly visible. It showed on the side of his forehead, outlined in the partial shape of the horseshoe. Small cuts were bleeding, but not seriously. Most of the damage was internal.

"Go fetch a plank and some more help to move him into the hall. Where is Sven?" Erik asked Bradan. Just then Tor came running and slid through the fence.

"Sven is in the cow barn helping a first-time cow with her calf. Shall I fetch him?" Caomh asked.

"Yes!"

"I...is P...Papa d...dead?" Tor sobbed.

"No, but his head is hurt badly. Run to tell your mother and have her send word to Father James and anyone else she thinks might help. We need a healer," Erik hurriedly told the young boy. Tor pivoted and headed for the hall at a dead run.

———

LATER THAT EVENING, several people had gathered in the bedroom where Harald lay unconscious in his straw bed. He had gotten rid of the feather bed he shared with his wife after she died. "I see no need for a fancy soft bed when there is no woman to share it with," he always said.

He lay there not moving but for an occasional twitch of a leg, a hand, or his mouth. His breathing was shallow, but regular. His heart rate had slowed and was weak. Father James had been praying silently and aloud ever since he arrived before sunset. Erik looked around the room, studying faces. Tor sat in a hard chair at the bedside gripping his papa's hand hoping for movement. The long wait proved too much, and he dozed off, laying his head on the bed next to the older man. Erna stood with her head bowed and a handkerchief held to her nose. She was in and out of silent prayer. Sven stood stoically against a wall with serious eyes glued on Harald's face. Father James looked as if his own father lay there unconscious. He was almost constantly mouthing prayers. Cinnia, the Irish house girl, was holding Gerna, rocking her in her arms, trying to keep the hungry toddler occupied. Occasionally, Erna would take up Gerna to give Cinnia a rest. Father James's surgeon was constantly feeling Harald's head, listening to his heart and breathing, never saying a word, just keeping a puzzled look on his face.

Lokhilla had been a sort of sorceress before she converted to Christianity, I wonder if she still knows any pagan healing skills. We must try everything. I wish Peluk were here right now. God, I have not thought about him in years! But I need a real healer— now! Erik berated himself for not acting sooner.

Erik eased his way over to his wife, Erna. "Do you think Lokhilla remembers any pagan healing spells?" he whispered into her ear.

"Are you serious?" Disbelief was painted on her face.

"I am willing to try anything. Father James is getting nowhere, and his 'approved' medical expert seems to know nothing. We have to do something quickly—head injuries can get bad very fast," Erik answered. "Please send someone after her, it can't hurt."

"Do you think Haakon would mind if she went back to the pagan ways?" she asked.

"Since he is off on a raid, we do not have time to wait to hear from him," Erik answered anxiously.

"All right, I will go myself so I can explain the situation to her."

"What about Gerna?"

"Cinnia can tend to her needs while I am gone. She should stay here—she is very worried about Papa."

It seemed to Erik that half the night had passed before Lokhilla showed up, when, in reality, it was less than two hours. She was dressed as a pagan sorceress with her gray-streaked dark-blond hair tied atop her head in loose braids sticking out in all directions, held in place with bone stick pins. A black leather dress that showed more skin than it covered was stretched tightly over her still-lithe frame. A leather cord hung around her neck adorned with human finger bones and bizarre-colored feathers. Her eyes were blue wells in a black mask of two large, painted diamonds. Red rivulets of ochre dribbled below her black eye makeup on white-grease-painted cheeks. On one finger was a tarnished silver wolf's head ring. A bracelet made of rings cut from human skull bones adorned one wrist. Black lightning streaks ran down each arm. A broach representing Loki was attached to the leather "X" between her ample, bare breasts. She looked like one of Satan's minions.

Father James stood up to protest. "What is that witch doing here? This is blasphemy!" he cried out.

Erik quickly strode over and grabbed him by

the elbow and escorted him from the room, across the great room of the hall, and out the main door. Sven followed close behind.

Quietly, but with force, Erik said, "I will try whatever I can to help Father out of this danger. Father grew up a pagan, so if pagan medicine is what he needs, that is what he will get. You and your surgeon have come up with nothing for hours, so I am trying another approach. You are welcome to stay, but you will keep your mouth shut! Do you understand?"

"You might have asked me before you invited her here looking like that, Erik," Sven said with bitterness in his voice.

"Erik, this is blasphemy. I cannot allow you to go through with this. If you insist, I cannot be a witness to it, and I will be forced to recommend excommunication for you. Do you understand me? The power of God far exceeds this silly pagan charade! You know that!" Father James was beside himself with anger.

"Yes, I know the power of God and have full faith in him. But if this 'pagan charade,' as you call it, helps Father come back to us, or even if it does not, I will know that I tried everything. He was a pagan long before he was a Christian, perhaps those old words will get his attention. That is all I am doing—I am not trying to ignore your authority. Can't you just understand that?" Erik was desperate for Harald's recovery. He looked over to Sven with pleading eyes. The younger brother seemed to catch on and nodded his approval.

"I..." Father James started.

"Erik! Your father speaks! Erna calls for you, now!" Cinnia yelled out the main hall door. Father James's jaw dropped, and his eyes bugged out. Erik released his arm as he and Sven sprinted to the bedroom where Harald lay, leaving Father James gaping on the stoop.

"Are you coming back in, Father?" Cinnia stood, holding the door open and tilting her head toward the bedroom.

Erna met Erik at the door. "Shortly after Lokhilla lit the incense and chanted a pagan prayer for health, he twitched, then he spoke your name. It came out slurred, but it was clear enough to be heard."

"I am here, Father." Erik had tears in his eyes.

Tor, still sitting by the bed holding Harald's hand, had fallen asleep, but was now wide awake. He looked hopefully up at Erik.

"Erik, that mast pole is too long for this knorr," Harald slurred. "Haakon, strike!...Woman, not now!...Sigurd! She is a thrall!...Father! Skræling...

Thorkell...don't stay!...Olaf..." Father James lifted an eyebrow at the mention of the saint king who had converted Norway to Christianity. Harald's words were gibberish, but at least he was speaking. He never opened his eyes or moved, other than the slight twitching that occurred at random all over his body. After a long pause, "Odin..." Father James winced and shook his head. Then "God Almighty!" his loudest outburst yet. Father James beamed. "Tor" was the next word.

"Papa!" Tor answered, surprised to hear his name.

"Bring Gerna," Erik said.

Erna handed him the sleeping toddler. Erik gently woke her up and asked her to say something to her papa. She sleepily looked at the man in the bed with his pale complexion and large bandage covering half his head and started crying uncontrollably. Erna quickly took her up and handed her to Cinnia who quickly carried her out the door.

"Dark..." Harald slurred, then seemed to relax. A moment later his legs twitched violently, and his breathing became labored. He arched, pulling his head back. His mouth opened followed by a long, scratchy exhale. His whole body then relaxed, and he was gone. Tor could not comprehend the stillness in his papa or the room. He looked around and saw only disbelief. Then everyone started crying, including his father.

Erik whispered, "It's...it's...over," between sobs.

Father James looked at Lokhilla with disdain, then went to Harald's head to bless his body. She looked at Erik, then Sven. It was difficult to read her expression with all the makeup on. She nodded to Sven and Erna, then quietly started out the door. Erna cut her off and whispered that she need not leave. Lokhilla answered that she would go clean up and come back in more appropriate attire. "What can I bring you?"

"Nothing at the moment. This all has to sink in." Erna quietly replied. The two women squeezed hands, and Lokhilla left the room.

———

THE FOLLOWING day several thralls from Erik's and Haakon's households prepared a plot in the family cemetery. Only obelisk-style stones for women and children were present. All the family men passing since Arg Ulfrson and the establishment of Ulfrstadt died as warriors. They had been cremated in pagan times on ships in the fjord. Harald's would be the first male Christian burial.

He had stipulated long ago that he would have a Christian burial and his mound would be rectangular rather than in the shape of a ship as was customary for someone of his status. "I spent more time in a hall than on a ship," he would say, whenever the subject came up.

A large rectangular grave was excavated to about knee deep, then a cut stone wall was erected to about shoulder high. Though a Christian burial forbade most of the possessions included in a pagan grave site, Harald's grave would be somewhat more extravagant than most. A flagstone floor was laid inside the rectangle and a raised cut stone platform to support the body was built in the middle. All was oriented in the traditional manner, facing east. A doorway and steps led out of the sunken floor on the east side. Once the body was interred, cut stones would fill the door and the whole rectangle would be filled with dirt. A rock with a horse head carved from solid granite would be placed above the door lintel as soon as it was finished. That would be several weeks away.

———

TWO DAYS LATER, nearly all of Ulfrstadt showed up at the new church on the village square to offer final respects to Jarl Harald Rolfcarlsson. After a ceremony at the church, a procession was led by Father James and his altar boys, followed by a horse-drawn caisson carrying Harald's body. The family members, a few Jarls from nearby Jarldoms, and finally, anyone wishing to follow, left the village and made their way up the hill to the west toward the family cemetery.

Harald had been dressed in his finest. Exquisitely tanned black leather boots adorned his feet. He had on handsomely woven gray wool trousers, an ivory-colored linen shirt, a red wool with black embroidered filigree-trimmed vest, and a blue-dyed wool tunic. Around his neck were one gold and one silver chain. The gold chain had a medallion of gold depicting a horse's head with a full, flowing mane. The silver chain bore a silver Christian Cross. A wool hat with gold and silver piping covered his head. A gold armlet was placed on each upper arm, and four gold bracelets were placed on each wrist. He had large gold rings on two fingers of each hand. A sword that once belonged to his grandfather decorated with gold inlays and etched filigree rested on his chest, the hilt under his crossed hands and the tip below his knees. His face had been painted white in a vain attempt to mask the terrible discoloration from his head wound.

Father James recited more prayers at the gravesite. Family members wept and said their goodbyes before the plank he was resting on in the caisson was transferred into the crypt. Next, a heavy linen cloth was placed over the body. The mourners slowly left the gravesite and made their way to Harald's Great Hall where a feast had been prepared. When all were gone, a stone worker placed the cut stones in the doorway to seal the crypt and a half dozen thralls began filling the crypt with dirt, a task that would take them until after the sun went down. After the dirt had time to settle, a cut stone roof would be added to seal the crypt.

Just as Erik and Sven were arriving at the hall, a conch shell ship's horn sounded out on the fjord. Rushing to the hillside, they looked out and, in the failing light, saw Haakon's *Dragon Fire* ship oars as it approached the dock. Still out on the water was Bjorn Ivarrson's *Wave Wolf*. *They're back early. Surely, they cannot have gotten word of Father's death soon enough to get here tonight. What brought them back?*

"You tend to the guests, I will go see what is afoot," Erik told Sven.

"Welcome home, Olaf, you are back early!" Erik greeted his cousin stepping off *Dragon Fire* onto Ulfrstadt's wooden plank dock.

"And you are dressed in fine clothes for

meeting a horde of warriors coming in from a raid," Olaf replied, noting Erik's fine wool black tunic and white linen shirt. "Where is everyone?"

"Yes, well...we are having a funeral feast in honor of my father in the hall up on the hill," Erik said, his voice failing.

"No, it cannot be!" Olaf exclaimed, astonished. "I return with my father's lifeless body after he was killed in a fight just south of York in Northumbria."

Tears filled Erik's eyes. "This is beyond belief! Father was kicked in the head by a horse four days past, just after the noon hour," Erik sobbed.

"Father met his fate that same day at the same time. A squad of about thirty English brigands surprised us as we rode along a road just on the outside of a forest some thirty leagues south of York. I have no idea what they were doing there. We were relaxed, believing there were no enemies anywhere nearby. They totally surprised us, but we managed to scatter them into the woods. Father had knocked one off his horse. Thinking the man was badly injured, Father got down to question him. It seems the man was only feigning injury because when Father approached, he rolled past Father, swinging his sword and drove it up into Father's back. Father staggered, stunned for a moment. By then, I had driven my sword down the man's neck, right into his chest. He died quickly. Father lingered for an hour or more."

"So sorry for your loss, cousin."

"And I for yours, cousin."

"We need to get you some help down here. I will return with help. You stay here with your father's corpse and your crew. I will get as many as I can. The mead may be flowing fast by now," Erik said, his voice reflected less than full confidence.

"You need to be with your family, and they need you right now," Olaf said, his voice as solid as he could make it.

"Your family is at Harald's Hall, too. I will tell them as discreetly as I am able," Erik stated.

"On second thought, I am coming with you," Olaf replied. "Bjarni, please take Father's body to his hall. I have some family business to tend to before returning. Have all my belongings taken there. I will explain later."

"As you wish, Olaf," Bjarni answered in a reverent tone.

———

TOGETHER THEY ENTERED the great hall of Jarl Harald Rolfcarlsson. By now the mood had shifted from somber mourning to jubilant celebration of the deceased's life. He had touched everyone in Ulfrstadt's lives in one way or another.

Harald's Great Hall could accommodate over a hundred people. The huge oak door opened into a great room sixty paces long and forty wide. The roof was supported by eight huge timbers that formed a rectangle forty paces long and twenty wide oriented north and south. The main door was on the east side. Near the rear support posts sat the great table, long enough for about thirty chairs on each side. The center chair had a high back with arms and was made of richly engraved oak. To this chair's left was a lesser, but still richly decorated, chair for the lady of the house. It had sat unused since the death of Harald's wife, nearly five years past. To the High Chair's right was another richly engraved albeit smaller chair. This was reserved for Harald's eldest son or some important guest, depending on the situation. Plain chairs were arranged all along both sides of the table. Down the center of the room and a few paces separated from the table, a central fire pit ran the length of the great table with the exception of an open space of about three paces in the center. Fire of various intensities ran along the fire pit on each side of the central opening. Smoke was drafted to the high peaked ceiling and out ventilation shafts, or chimneys, along the center of the roof beam. From the large oak door to the main table was a clear space where visitors or those with business could approach the center of the table unhindered. Various animal parts were being roasted in some locations along the fire pit, others left open for heating the room or for light.

What set Harald's Hall apart from similar ones was that no great antlered animals adorned the wall behind the High Chair. Where Haakon had elk, stag, and ice bear heads decorating his wall, Harald's was decorated with a giant tapestry chronicling the family's history since the founding of Ulfrstadt.

The tapestry was woven by Harald's wife, Astrid, and was a source of pride for him. It depicted a wild wolf coming out of the forest, mating with a landsman's wife. The offspring resulting from that union was named Arg. Arg claimed he was sired by a wild wolf and named himself Arg Ulfrsson. He became a great warrior in the service of Olaf Triggvisson, who united all of Norway into a Christian kingdom. Arg was appointed Jarl and awarded a great piece of land he named Ulfrland. The tapestry went on to show the building of houses and ships, the sailing of armed men, marriages, arrival of offspring, and other significant family events. The succession of the Jarldom of Ulfrland chronicled Arg Wolfson,

Carl Argsson, Rolf Carlsson, Rolfcarl Rolfsson, and Harald Rolfcarlsson. All siblings of the Jarls were also displayed. The last depiction was the birth of Tor, son of Erik, seven years earlier, before Astrid's health began to fail. Harald forbade anyone else from working on the tapestry after Astrid's death, even though Gerna had been born and Sven had taken a wife.

Erik's wife, Erna, was skilled with the loom and could make beautiful tapestries herself. Harald adamantly said that no one else will touch Astrid's work. Erna's work was displayed on the north wall, depicting the family events from Astrid's death to the present.

The roasting meat and warm light given off by the fire pit and torches attached to the support posts provided an inviting atmosphere. Along the table were large wooden and metal platters holding various pieces of cooked meat. In front of the High Chair, which was now reserved for Erik, sat a silver platter with beef ribs sticking up. Other platters were heaped with beef, hog, lamb, goat, goose, chicken, and fresh fish. Still others displayed various breads, cheese, carrots, cabbages, beets, radishes, and other vegetables. Mead or wine filled every cup.

Loud conversation was sometimes accented with laughter along the main table and other smaller tables set up around the great room. Many people were standing along the walls and between tables. People were hoisting drinking cups, but none were eating. Sven was walking around the room, trailed by his young bride, Unndis, Erna, Tor, and Gerna greeting the throngs of mourners. Seated at the great table to the right of the empty family seats were Haakon's wife, Lokhilla, Olaf's wife, Skjoldis, Dagna, Olaf's daughter, and Bjarni's wife, Nordis. Filling drinking cups with wine and mead were Cinnia and other thralls of Harald's household and those of Haakon's.

When Erik and Olaf walked in, the entire hall fell completely silent. Fearing something terrible might happen, Gerna started crying. After a quick look around, Olaf went straight to his mother. Lokhilla looked at his war tunic, splattered with old blood and knew the news was bad without even looking at his tortured face.

He leaned over the table and whispered in her ear. She immediately began shaking and tears flowed over her face as he explained what had happened. Skjoldis stood up, tears filling her eyes, muscular arms rippling as her fists knotted, Dagna started crying and reached for her mother. Nordis shook her head, wondering the fate of the rest of the crew. She soon learned that two others were killed and two more had minor injuries. Only Haakon's body was returned to Norway for burial.

Before long, the news had spread throughout the hall, and the mood turned more somber. Losing two great lords in a week was hard to fathom. Most stood around in stunned silence. Father James let out a painful moan and headed straight for Olaf and Lokhilla. The frightful 'witch' he had feared three nights past was now an elegant but tragic victim.

"Friends," Erik began, "upon learning of the loss of my uncle, I must ask that this funeral celebrating my father's life be brought to an end now. The family will distribute the food throughout the households of Ulfrstadt by the end of tomorrow. In the meantime, we ask that you leave us alone at this time while we grieve the loss of my dear uncle. Thank you."

Maids began to clear the food from the main table.

"Let us get back to your ship and tend to what needs to be done there before going to Ha...your hall," Erik said as he took Olaf's elbow.

OLAF PULLED AWAY. "Your place is here, Erik. Bjarni is taking care of the ship. I will tend to Mother.

Your family can help us with the arrangements when you have everything under control here. Father James, will you accompany us? I believe your words may comfort Mother."

Bjarni had put Haakon's body in the ice house behind the great hall. Before leaving England, Olaf had cleaned Haakon's body, put his limbs in the burial position, and wrapped the body in a wool blanket. When the family members entered the main hall, Bjarni jumped up from his seat at the end of Haakon's great table and hurried to Olaf to report he had accomplished all that was requested of him. Olaf told him he should go to his own home to console his wife. Bjarni told Olaf that crew members were taking care of everything on the *Dragon Fire*.

———

THE NEXT DAY, thralls from both houses, led by instructions from Erik, began preparing a crypt for Haakon's body. It was laid out in the shape of a ship oriented with the bow to the east. It was to be constructed of cut rocks just as Harald's had been. Other than shape and location, the two graves were very much alike. A marker stone was ordered to be cut from solid gray granite about shoulder high and two hands thick. On its face would be a carving in Haakon's likeness holding a sword and standing on the bow deck of a longship at full sail and manned by a crew of Norse warriors.

Three days later a second entire funeral procession and celebration were repeated in Haakon's Hall. This time the only ship's horn was part of the service.

CHAPTER 15
JARLS

"Father, how is it that you will now be Jarl of Ulfrland?" Tor asked Erik a few days after it was announced that Erik would become the Jarl after Jarl Harald Rolfcarlsson had passed away.

"I know you have been schooled on the succession of titles according to the laws of Norway nobility, my son," Erik replied in a stern voice.

"Yes, but it seems like it is always old men who become Jarls. You do not even have any gray hairs yet, Father. You seem too young to be a Jarl. And why are there Jarls in our family in the first place?" Tor responded.

"Now, I know you have learned our family history, so you can answer that question yourself!" Erik admonished his son.

"But the story of Arg Ulfrsson sounds like a make-believe story. More a legend than truth. How would a 'make-believe' person be given a great land holding? Then be named Jarl? I am bewildered by that." Tor had obviously been pondering the subject deeply.

"When Harald Finehair was fighting to unite all the petty kingdoms under one flag, he was looking for fierce leaders. Jarl Arg was not a jarl at the time. But he fought with incredible ferocity and cunning. Men watched him and followed him bravely into battle. Under his leadership, the men in this part of Norway helped Finehair unite many of the coastal lands. Once the country was united, King Harald Finehair ceded what is now Ulfrland, though it was several smaller kingdoms at the time, to Arg Ulfrsson as payment for his loyalty.

"Under Norwegian law, a Jarl is succeeded by his eldest son. If the eldest son is deceased, cannot, or will not perform the duties as Jarl, the next eldest son becomes the new Jarl. A few times, there has been no son to pass the office on to. In most of those cases, the office of Jarl is passed on to a cousin or other relatives. In a few cases, the office has been passed on to a female heir. Those have been few and are generally a short-term solution," Erik explained in his best "father" voice.

"So, a wild man could come down out of the

mountains, claim he is the son of a bear, defeat all of our warriors, drive us out our Hall, and the king could name him Jarl and take all we have and give it to this wild man?" Tor asked seriously.

"For an eight-year-old, you do have a vivid imagination! But technically, I suppose that could happen. I would not lose any sleep over it if I were you, however. Did I answer your question to your satisfaction?" Erik asked his son.

"I still do not see how a man could claim he is the son of a wild wolf, and a king would believe him." Tor shook his head as he looked at the teacup in his hands.

"I think you are old enough to hear this part of the story," Erik proclaimed.

Tor looked questioningly at his father's face.

"The truth is that Arg was the son of a poor farmer named Gorm. He had little ambition for anything but drinking vast quantities of mead. Arg was a dreamer and wanted to do great things. But since Gorm never did anything to gain anyone's respect, no one gave Arg a chance to prove himself.

"Then, Harald Finehair's men came through recruiting warriors to fight in his army to unite all of Norway. Arg jumped at the chance to make a name for himself as a fighter. Of course, all that knew him laughed at his ambition. That was when he made up the story about being sired by a wild wolf. In the days and weeks to come, he fought like a wolf and made a name for himself. Soon enough he had a following, and his men made a big difference in uniting the country. When he was made king, Olaf rewarded Arg for his actions. Our family, of course, is directly descended from Arg, so the Jarldom remains in our name," Erik said with pride.

"Yes, that finally answers my question, Father. Thank you for telling me the truth," Tor responded.

CHAPTER 16
TOR ERIKSON

Dressed in a padded wool "suit of armor" wielding a light shield and wooden sword, Tor stood two paces in front of Thorm Bjarnisson. Thorm had seen ten winters and Tor nine. This would be Tor's first practice combat with wooden weapons. He has passed the training drills and was ready for his first test of those skills. Thorm had advanced to the use of real weapons, but since this was Tor's first go, he would use the younger trainees' weapons. Thorm looked forward to putting the Jarl's son in his place.

"So, the cowardly Jarl's cowardly son has come out to see what being a real man is about.'I'll make sure you wish you had never come to the training," Thorm taunted the younger Tor.

"My father is no coward, and neither am I," Tor responded.

"Your father is a sniveling, Skræling-loving coward who has never set foot on a battlefield!" Thorm exclaimed, pushing the younger boy's anger.

"You may begin your combat when you are ready. Remember this is only training. No one is to get hurt. Just reinforce what you have learned about thrusting, blocking, and parrying," Gorm, the instructor admonished the boys.

Thorm did not hesitate before he stepped forward and slammed his wood sword down into Tor's exposed shoulder at the base of his neck. Tor went down in a heap, dropped his sword, and moved his hand to his hurting shoulder. Thorm stood over him with a menacing smile on his face, pushed the point of his sword into Tor's exposed neck and asked, "Yield?"

"Yield." Tor grimaced.

"That was easy," Thorm said as he turned toward the instructor.

"You may be excused," Gorm told Thorm, then kneeled on one knee to check on Tor's injury.

"Are you all right, Tor?" Gorm inquired.

"It hurts, but not too bad. I feel like a fool," Tor replied.

"I think Thorm holds a grudge of some kind

against you. I have not heard him taunting other boys like did did you."

"I want to fight him again tomorrow," Tor said forcefully.

"I am not sure that is a good idea. You will still be sore, and he will punish you harder," Gorm replied. "I should have paired you with a smaller opponent for your first combat."

"No, I should have seen it coming. In a battle, a warrior does not get to choose the size of his foe. I will fight him tomorrow and teach him some humility," Tor stated with finality.

"I believe it is better to have your fight here, under my eye, than letting you go out of here and fight with real weapons. I don't want the Jarl's son severely wounded under my eye, but it is better than him being killed outside this school," Gorm conceded.

The next day, dressed as the day before, Tor stood before Thorm. Tor made a point of not saying a word about yesterday's debacle to his father.

"I can't believe you came back for more punishment," Thorm goaded Tor with a sardonic grin on his ten-year-old face.

Tor just looked up at him and raised his shield slightly.

"You may begin your combat when you are

ready. Remember the goal here is to learn, not to hurt each other." Gorm glared into Thorm's eyes when he made the warning about injuries.

Thorm had never taken his eyes from Tor, not picking up Gorm's nonverbal threat. He felt that since Tor asked for this fight, he was free to deliver as much pain as he wanted.

Thorm started with a brutal slash at Tor's shield. Tor surprised Thorm when he sidestepped the attack and struck Thorm painfully across his back with the blade of his sword. Infuriated, Thorm jerked around and went after Tor a second time. Tor was ready, and when Thorm raised his arm to smash Tor with his sword, Tor slammed the blade of his sword into Thorm's armpit. The pain caused Thorm to drop his sword.

Thorm, grimacing, reached down to pick up his sword. Tor stepped on the hilt and drove his shield into Thorm's, knocking him off his feet. Tor quickly stood over Thorm and pressed his blade to Thorm's neck.

"Yield?" Tor asked forcefully. Gorm just closed his eyes and nodded. Tor did not gloat, just turned to Gorm and released a long breath.

"You certainly learn fast, young Tor," Gorm exclaimed, then helped a totally embarrassed Thorm to his feet.

"This is not over. You got lucky. You're still a

sniveling coward, and your father is still a sniveling, murderous coward and Skræling lover!" Thorm snarled.

"Why do you call my father a murderer?" Tor asked Thorm.

"My father was on that Greenland trip. He watched your pitiful father murder his shipmate. Father even pulled your Skræling-loving father from Tyrkir's bloody body. That was a cowardly act."

"Tyrkir's death was justified when he unrepentantly murdered the crippled Skræling who was just trying to stop Tyrker from stealing his family's possessions. He was shouting "NO" in Norse so the warrior would understand. Tyrkir knew Peluk and knew he was harmless. Killing him was a hate-filled and needless act. My father reacted. The killing was justified!" Tor exclaimed.

"Lies! Father was there and saw it all!" Thorm yelled as he threw down his shield.

Gorm stepped between the boys, saying, "That is enough! I will hear no more of this in this school. Both of you are dismissed, and don't come back until you are ready to be civil. You are here to learn skills that may keep you alive in combat, not settle old scores that have nothing to do with either of you! Now, get out of my sight, both of you!"

When Tor trudged up the hill toward Erik's

Hall, Erik spotted him from the horse pens, noting his drooping shoulders and scowl on his face. Erik dropped what he was doing and confronted Tor.

"What is wrong, son?" Erik inquired.

Tor was flummoxed. He wanted to believe his father was none of the things Thorm accused him of, but a seed of doubt had been planted.

"What is the truth, Father? Did you murder Tyrkir on that Greenland voyage?"

"What makes you ask that, and why are you back so early from your combat training? I thought you liked it?" Erik fired questions back at Tor.

"Yesterday I was pitted against Thorm Bjar-nisson. He started trying to get me off-guard by accusing you of being a coward and a Skræling lover. With one swing of his sword, he put me down and defeated me. I swore that would not happen again and went back to face him again today. I was afraid of what would happen. But this time I beat him easier than I thought I could. After he yielded, he said you are still a murdering, Skræling-loving coward. He went on to say that you have never stepped onto a battlefield, and his father was on that voyage and witnessed you murder Tyrkir because of a filthy Skræling. I defended you, and he replied those were all lies. Now, I want the truth!" Tor pleaded.

"I understand your concern, son. I have told

you the events of that day on that island off Hella-land. It happened the way I said it did. It was a day I prefer not to remember, but it is as clear in my memory as if it happened yesterday. By the time we reached Hellaland, everyone aboard that ship knew Peluk and that he was no warrior. Tyrkir was in the party that found us on the ice and brought us back to the ship. He knew all about Peluk and his physical limitations.

"He killed the boy out of unwarranted hate. I could not let that stand. I wanted to punish him. I admit, I did lose my mind temporarily. I guess if Bjarni wants to say it was murder, that is his right. I cannot control what he thinks. But Haakon told me that once Bjarni killed a shipmate who acci-dently killed a man who had saved Bjarni's life. Both killings occurred in a pitched and confusing battle."

"What should I do about Thorm?" Tor asked in a calmer voice.

"All you can do is tell him what I have told you and let him decide for himself. As far as not going to battle, I have built warships that carry our warriors into battle. But I chose not to go on raids that are for the purpose of killing, stealing, and capturing slaves. In a war defending our home-land, I will be in the front lines. And I do not care who hears that from me," Erik replied.

"Thank you, Father," Tor answered.

Tor and Thorm entered into an uneasy truce that lasted until Thorm got into a fight with an older boy outside of Gorm's combat class and killed the older boy when he stuck a knife in his belly. The killing was ruled self-defense and justified. Oddly, Thorm always had an excuse for not going on raids in foreign lands. Tor took his father's lesson to heart and never dreamed of going on raids into foreign lands with other Norsemen.

CHAPTER 17
TWO SHIPS

After Haakon's death, Olaf lost interest in raiding himself. He sent his ships full of eager young men and boys, but he could never find the time to go along. As luck would have it, Erik was contracted to build two large longships for a lord who resided in Bergen. It would take nearly a half a year to complete them. Olaf partnered with Erik to fulfill the contract.

When completed, the *Water Wolf* and the *Black Dragon* would be magnificent warships. Seventy ells long, twenty wide, they would need to be built to slide though the water at great speed and to handle the rough seas along the East Coast of England and sail far up the rivers. Sixteen oars, two men per oar, on each side would propel them in still waters and in river channels faster than any

ships afloat. They would carry eighty men in full
battle gear.

———

"WE MUST FIND JUST the right trees to build these
magnificent ships." Erik looked at Tor, who was
trying to look manly as he urged his pony to keep
up with the big horses the adults were riding. Olaf
and the shipwright, Hjalmar, accompanied Erik
and Tor on this morning. "We are searching, in
particular, for oaks deep in gullies that have grown
tall and straight with limbs only near the top to
reach the sun with their branches and leaves. Also,
four special trees are sought that grow from the
sides of gullies so that their trunks came out of the
ground on the steep slopes and curved upward
such that they have just the right diameter and
curve to form the bow and stern keels of the ships.
The wood is stronger if it grows to that shape,
rather than the tedious process of softening and
bending the wood after it is cut. We also seek a few
pines higher on the uplands with huge trunks that
would have slow, dense growth at their bases from
which to make *the old woman*, or mast base, for
each ship." Erik gestured to general areas to make
his points.

"Once the proper trees are selected and

marked, crews will be sent into the forest to cut them down, size the proper logs, and haul them to the shipworks on the beach. We want the trees at the shipworks by the late spring and early summer so that we can begin building as soon as possible," Erik spoke to Tor as a teacher would speak to a student.

Tor often accompanied the men on these forays into the forest and always listened intently. Even at his young age he wanted to learn as much as he could about the ship building process.

While Erik and Olaf busied themselves with the warship order, Sven occupied himself with the animal husbandry and crop production side of the farm. It was a good and profitable arrangement for all.

"Father, won't those big trees break when you cut them down? They are so tall, and they must be heavy. I know I would break if I fell that far!" Tor observed, craning his neck to look up to the tops of the tall trees.

Hjalmar jumped into the conversation. "Good question, young Tor. To solve that problem, we cut all these small trees and brush to get them out of the way. We use them to make a big pile right where the big trees will fall so that there is a soft 'cushion' when the toppled tree lands. All this small stuff will be carried back to the shipworks.

Some will be used to make bark rope, some boiled for the sap for water proofing. The bigger stuff will be used to make charcoal that we need for smelting bog iron."

Erik picked up the explanation. "While the logs are being harvested, peat harvested from the bogs will be roasted for hours to drive off the moisture. Once dried, the iron nodules will be brought to the kilns at the shipworks. The kilns are those short clay shafts, about knee-high to a man, cut into the bank next to the gravel beach of the fjord. The shafts are lined with a layer of clay, silt, sand, and horse manure, then fire-dried to create a hard furnace for the smelting process." Erik beamed with pride while explaining the process to his son.

"Once the kilns are ready, charcoal and the peat nodules will be burned for hours. A bellows is attached near the bottom of the kiln, or shaft furnace, to blow fresh air into the charcoal to make the fire hotter. The hotter the fire, the purer the iron will be. The iron settles from the top where even amounts of charcoal and peat nodules are added at intervals. Eventually, a slag bloom is created at the bottom of the furnace. The lower section of the furnace shaft is opened so the slag bloom can be removed and taken over to the smithy your grandfather built a few years past as part of the shipworks."

"How do they make things from that blob of hot stuff from the furnace?" Tor asked.

"The slag blooms are heated until they glow, separated, and folded over and over again, then beat with a hammer to drive out impurities, improving the quality of the finished metal. Your grandfather had built a reputation for producing fine iron products, and I learned from him, keeping the family reputation intact. The more pure the iron is, the better the finished products will be. The smithy has an anvil stone of the hardest red granite and its own charcoal furnace so the metal can be reheated as often as necessary. Iron bars pounded out on that anvil had been valuable trade goods for your grandfather. Now the smithy will be engaged in producing nails, rivets, rivet washers, and all the other metal components for building the warships," Erik continued.

"As soon as the wood is brought in, production will begin by cutting keels for each ship. That one big oak we marked will make the bottom keel board for both ships. In this case, that would be sixty ells long." Erik pointed it out to Tor.

"Look here, lord!" Hjalmar shouted from up the gully where he and Olaf had wandered while Erik was instructing Tor. "We have found a gold mine! These four trees and the ground they grow from slipped down this hill several years past, tilting them downward. In the years after, the trunks bent and grew toward the sky. These trees make perfect bow and stern posts with no bending needed. I never saw four more perfect trees growing this close together. Amazing!"

————

A WEEK LATER, several cut logs had been delivered to the shipworks. "First an axe and an adze will be used to square the logs. The scraps from this process will be used to make charcoal, as we have already talked about. We will end up with a modified T-shaped log sixty ells long, two hands wide on top and tapering sharply to one hand wide, that is carried three hands wide to the bottom. We will make one for each ship. A draw knife and wide chisel are next used to smooth all sides of the keel boards." Erik demonstrated the process using hand gestures and scraps of wood that had been cut from previous projects.

"Next, chisels, axes, adzes, and draw knives are used to shape a four-ell long scarf into each end of the keel boards. The forward scarf will be made so the prow keel post board is on the outside. The aft scarf will have the bottom keel board as the long one.

"After the keel boards are complete, they will

be painted with several coats of boiled pine pitch to waterproof them on all sides. The pine pitch is harvested from live trees by cutting a diagonal slit through the bark on one side of a healthy pine, fir, or spruce tree. The sap collected in this manner will not kill the tree.

"Next, six-ell sections of the large diameter upland trees are cut and split. They are shaped to a two-hand wide flat side to fit the top of the keel board. Then, a concave shape is made from there to fit the flattening of the bottom of the ship above the keel. This large diameter log is known as *the old woman* and will serve as a socket for the base of the mast. It will also provide ballast to the bottom of the ship. The top of the old woman is rounded and tapered toward the front of the ship. In the center of the old woman is cut a round pit three hands across and four hands deep to accept the base of the mast. From the outer-most edge of the aft side of the round hole, a wedge -shaped slot is removed and the wood set aside. Once the mast is set, this wedge is to be replaced and held in place by removable fasteners to allow the lowering of the mast when needed. All surfaces of the old woman are then painted with the boiled pine pitch and dried." Erik did not tire while explaining the process to Tor, who struggled to focus on what his father demonstrated.

"Once dry, the old woman is placed in the center of the keel board. The fit and location is carefully marked so that the mast would be centered in the ship, and then it is removed. Now, a paste of boiled and thickened pine pitch is spread over the adjoining surfaces and the old woman *is* returned to its permanent location. Holes are bored through the old woman down into the keel board and boiled pine pitch coated oak treenails are driven into the holes. Once all the pine pitch is dried, *the old woman* and the keel board will be joined and strong, as if they are carved from the same piece of wood.

"Next, the bow and stern keel boards are shaped and smoothed in the same manner as the bottom keel board from those special curved logs we harvested. Temporary supports are set up to hold the end keel boards vertically in place. Again, the keel pieces are glued with boiled and thickened pine tar and pinned together with wood rivets. The wood rivets are made by driving a treenail all the way through both pieces being joined. The ends of the treenails are cut smooth with the surface. Next, a chisel is used to make a small slit in each end of the treenail. Then, a small wedge is driven into each end at the same time, spreading the ends, making a permanent, tight joint. The T-shaped inside edges of the end keel posts are tapered quickly as the shape of the keel changes from horizontal to vertical. By the time the waterline was reached, the keel board is flat and square. Once those are in place for both ships, they are ready to start attaching the strakes which will form the hulls and give the ships their strength."

"Building ships is hard, and you have to know a lot of things," Tor said as he looked around the busy shipworks. Some men were busy smelting iron, others splitting logs. The smithy was pounding out and shaping nails.

And on it went, day after day Erik would go straight for the shipworks in the morning and return to the hall after dark. Tor would join him after his daily chores were completed. Tor witnessed and helped where possible in the shaping of strakes, ribs, and other wooden parts for the ships. He spent as little time in the hot, smelly smithy as necessary learning how the nails, rivets, and other metal components were made. Erik patiently showed Tor every step along the way while the two ships slowly took shape.

Tor was mesmerized with the strake making process as Erik explained while the workmen were engaged. "First, the log is split down the middle, making two half logs. Then, those are split, making quarter logs. Again, the quarter logs are split. This way we can make eight or more strakes from one log. See how each strake is split off with axes and wedges at one and one-half hands thick and tapering to two fingers thick. The inside is shaped by marking the locations of the ship's ribs, two ells apart. Each strake is made for a specific place on the hull, so the rib locations change slightly as the strakes run from the keel to the gunwale...and so on until a big supply of strakes are shaped.

"I want you to watch as I smooth and shape this rough-cut strake. In this case, we will make the tenth strake thicker because that is the water-line and takes the most stress from the waves. Also, the fourteenth strake is thicker because it is where the oar ports will be located. It must take the strain of the oars pulling against it. Those strakes will also be strengthened by adding an oak knee on the both sides of the oar ports to reduce the wear." Erik liked to smooth the strakes after they had been rough-shaped. The tedious job of pulling the draw knife along the grain of the strake boards gave him time to reminisce about his relationship with his father. That relationship had been strained before Erik's voyage to Greenland with his uncle, Haakon.

Erik explained the family history to Tor. "Papa had a terrible voyage to Greenland. I was made to stay in Norway because I was only three years old. Your great-grandfather had gone with Thorfinn

Thorkellsson to Vinland in an effort to establish a trade partnership with the Skræling and explore for a permanent settlement in that country. Something had gone wrong, and a fight broke out.

"A few of the Norse sailors had returned with Skræling arrows still embedded in their torsos. Your great-grandfather, Rolfcarl Carlsson, had one of those arrows just under his ribs on his right side. The bleeding had been stopped with a woolen plug, but the stone arrow point and a bit of the shaft were left in his flesh. In the days it took them to return to Brattalid, the wound began to fester. Two days later, Papa Harald's father passed.

"He was buried in Greenland near the grave of Eric the Red, a distant cousin. His grave was simple, marked only with a single stone. Eric's eldest son, Leif, adheres strictly to Christian burial customs, and with Eric the Red deceased, he rules Greenland. Papa Harald was severely traumatized by the events and returned to Norway and vowed never to leave the homeland again." Erik's eyes lost focus as a sad expression dominated his face.

His demeanor lightened as he started talking about his father's accomplishments. "Instead, he became renowned for producing some of the best wool, beeves, sheep, and horses in Norway. In addition, he expanded these shipworks, and his crews built knorrs for traders plying the open seas as well as fishing and small transport boats used on the fjords and coast. Your grandfather wanted me to follow in his shoes, to shun the typical Norse vocation of raiding and pillaging helpless peasants and monasteries in foreign lands. 'Hard work pays the soul far more than pilfering helpless peasants,' he would say when trying to convince me not to train with my cousin Olaf in the use of weapons of war. In spite of his efforts, I had become competent with bow, sword, and axe."

I must not allow my own fears and feelings to interfere with Tor's choices. I do not want to alienate him as Father did me. I learned so many things on that Greenland voyage. Hmm...I guess ship building techniques were included... he thought, as he pulled the draw knife in short strokes in line with the wood grain to achieve a smooth surface on the outside of the long strake board.

Yes, the Greenland voyage was the turning point in our relationship. It was not the danger that changed me; it was mainly the way the rest of the crew treated Peluk. Even Olaf could not understand me, or why I defended the little Skræling. But that kind of blind cruelty and hate is foolishness. The boy was harmless, with his bad arm and size, he was no threat to anyone. Yet, there he was...unafraid to go after that big bear with one arm and a little spear. And he did not run away when he saw the Norsemen approaching. Even after…well, probably every person he was ever close to was killed in that storm, and he kept right on going. He performed that funeral for his grandmother, and then tried to protect his family's belongings from us. Remarkable bravery when confronted with such disaster.

I came to appreciate Father's point of view after that. Peluk taught me that you do the right thing until you are unable to do anything. It is the same thing Father always used to say about hard work producing something beats stealing it every time. It just makes you feel better. I must convey this way of thinking to Tor before he falls in with the 'Let's go raiding!' crowd. Erik's expression remained far away from the present.

Thinking on it, Father must have done some soul-searching too. He showed no anger or vengefulness that I slipped out and went on the voyage with Haakon, despite his feelings on the matter. He just took up with me like I had been working side by side with him all along.

Although it was a bit of a surprise, I must say, when he told me that I would be getting married on the coming fall equinox. I had less than two months to prepare! My bride would be the daughter of a stockman from Bergen whom I had never met. The bride price agreed on was three broken horses, including a bred mare, and a milk cow. Oh well, she has been well worth that and more. Tor is a fine son who is dutiful and hard-working. And little Gerna is a prize in any man's house. Yes, Father married me well. I wonder if she feels the same? I should ask her...sometime. Another strake done! Where has the day gone? Engrossed in his thoughts, Erik forgot he was trying to explain things to Tor, who had gotten bored with Erik's silence and wandered off.

———

AFTER SEVERAL MORE DAYS OF intense instruction, Erik thought Tor must be overwhelmed and asked, "This is a lot of information. Do you understand all I have said so far?" On the table before him in a shed laid rough drawings showing all the things Erik had been describing and showing his son.

"I think I understand, but building a ship is harder than building a wagon! Papa showed me how that works," Tor replied.

"Shall I continue, or have you had enough for today?" Erik asked.

"Tell me the rest, then I want to see more being made so I learn it better," Tor replied eagerly.

"Blocks will be installed along the top strakes on both sides and a batten placed on the outside of those blocks. The warriors' shields will be placed in that rail between the blocks just before the ships

205

go into battle. Various cleats will be added along the inside for attaching sail lines and other needed ropes. Aft, on the right outside, a large cone-shaped block will be installed just above the waterline. This is called a *tit*."

"Why is it called a *tit*?" Tor asked.

"Well...it looks kind of like a pig's tit when she is suckling piglets, I guess," Erik replied.

"I saw Mother's tit when she was suckling Gerna, and it sort of looked like that," Tor said matter-of-factly.

"It would probably be better if you don't tell your mother her tit looks like a pig's tit," Erik cautioned Tor with a smirk.

The instruction, questions, and hard work went on all summer, fall, and into the winter. "By the time these ships are ready for putting in the water, the owner and his crews will be here to man them. These ships will be used by Hrjorolf Gramarsson and his Shieldmaiden wife, Gerdis Hrjolfswife, when he accompanies the king's invasion of England in the spring, so we must have them ready and seaworthy by then," Erik instructed.

"Will you be going to war, or cousin Olaf?" Tor asked anxiously.

"No, I am no warrior, and your second cousin Olaf lost interest in fighting when he watched his father killed in a worthless skirmish with some outlaws." Bitterness was evident in Erik's voice. "Together Olaf and I will build more ships if we get any more orders, and help Sven run this farm. Several of Olaf's freemen will be sailing for the king in Olaf's *Dragon Fire*, though. In another week, these ships will be taking shape, if I get back to work. Do you want to help me with shaping these last few strake boards or help Ivar with shaping rib pieces?"

"I want to help Ivar—he wants to show me how to use the block plane," Tor replied and headed to a tent where Ivar had a stack of rib pieces rough-cut and ready for final shaping and smoothing. *The final shaping of the ribs will take place once all the strake boards are in place. Each rib has a specific place along the hull and is cut flat at the deck level. Once the deck boards are in place, the ribs are continued up to the rail on the inside of the top strake,* Tor remembered what Erik had told him.

A few weeks later, both ships stood anchored in the harbor, ready for the crews to arrive from Bergen.

CHAPTER 18

THORKELL ARRIVES IN ULFRSTADT

After Erik had sold the two longships to Hrjorolf Gramarsson, he had had only one order for a new, small coastal trader over the next couple of years. The farm production became the main economy for Erik, Sven, and Olaf. The port of Ulfrstadt had slowed in growth. It seemed to Erik that much of the trade was for Greenlandic wool and ivory. The slowing economy was sending more young men to fight in foreign lands.

One day, while practicing his carving skills at the quiet shipworks, Tor heard a ship's conch shell horn. Ships arriving had become an unusual event in day-to-day life in Ulfrstadt. He was happy to have a diversion.

By the time the ship's sail was lowered, Erik

stopped to tell Tor it was his uncle from Green-land. "Come, let us give Uncle Thorkell a hardy welcome. He has two boys about your age."

"Welcome to Ulfrstadt, Uncle. We have fresh mead, and Sven is slaughtering a cow right now. A feast is in order!" Erik had not seen Thorkell since his own trip to Greenland eleven years past. Harald and Haakon had both died, leaving Thorkell as the last of the Rolfcarlsson brothers. Thorkell's planned trip to Norway, ten years past, had to be canceled due to the arrival of his twin boys.

Tor noted that Thorkell was dressed in fine black wool trousers and a blue wool tunic trimmed with white filigree around the collar. A wide black leather belt circled his waist, and his feet were clad in good leather boots albeit they were crusted with salt residue from his voyage. Tor felt rather shabby in his worn trousers and dirty shirt with holes in the elbows.

"It is not with good cheer that I came on this voyage, Erik. I need to meet with you, Sven, and Olaf as soon as it can be arranged," Thorkell replied.

"Olaf is in the forest, marking trees for a lumber sale. We can talk at dinner tonight in the main hall on the farm, if that is satisfactory. You sound troubled, is there something you need?" Erik asked.

"Let us go get some of your mead, we'll talk later. Is this your boy?" He reached out and hugged the boy. "This one will be big and strong, eh?" Thorkell was all smiles.

"Glad to make your acquaintance, Great-Uncle. My name is Tor Eriksson," Tor said, showing respect for the older man.

"And polite, too!" Thorkell addressed Erik.

"His mother tries to raise him right. He only gets in trouble with his father and second cousin Olaf," Erik chided, poking Tor with his foot.

———

THAT EVENING they sat at the main table in the great hall on the hill overlooking Ulfrstadt. Olaf's hall and Father James's church were the only other large buildings in the town. Several booths lined irregular short streets where merchants hawked everything from iron bars to ells of linen cloth. These days it seemed that half of the booths stood empty most of the year. Several small houses stretched out to the south from the center of town. A few small fields for growing vegetables lay on the outskirts and beyond those were some barley fields. Peat bogs filled the wetter parts of the valley floor. Steep foothills rose on both sides of the river valley which gave way to the mountains beyond.

At the great table, they enjoyed horn cups of fresh mead. Thorkell met Erna and Gerna for the first time, as well as Sven and his new wife, Dagna. Dagna was showing her first pregnancy. On the roasting hearth were fresh cuts of beef. The hall smelled of roasting beef and fresh-cut summer flowers.

"While the pleasure of your company is untold, womenfolk, I must have some privacy with Erik, Sven, and Olaf if you do not mind," Thorkell said at last, his belly bulging from the hearty meal.

"What is it, Uncle?" Erik inquired with concern in his voice. Olaf turned his attention to Thorkell.

"As you know, business in Greenland is booming. My farm in the western settlements is beyond description. I have unlimited pasture for cattle, horses, sheep, and goats. As you know, our wool is renowned for its fine quality. And the exotic furs, walrus ivory and meat, and ice bear products cannot be beat." The older man paused. His sad expression told the younger men that something was tearing him apart.

"Here is my problem, I am getting old and have lost my heirs." Tears welled in his eyes. "My boys, Gunnar and Helgi, were fishing last fall when a sudden storm blew in out of nowhere. Their boat capsized, and they, along with two peasant boys, were lost." He took a minute for that to sink in. It was news to Erik, Olaf, and Sven. Their expressions reflected their shock and dismay.

Thorkell regained his composure and said, "I know the economy of Europe, and Norway especially, is slowed right now. But Greenland is enjoying the best of times, and there is nothing to make us think that will change any time soon. The climate keeps getting better for growing self-sown wheat and raising livestock. We have even had some success trading with those northern Skræling. The ones you talked about, Erik." He paused for a minute.

"Now, with my boys gone, and your fathers have both passed, I am asking if one, or two, of you might consider coming to Greenland. I am getting old and need to slow down some. I can set you both up on large spreads and get you started with your own livestock. Of course, you can bring your own as well.

"Leif Eriksson and his brother have been trading for lumber from the southern Skræling, so we have a modest supply of that now, too. My understanding from our earlier talk here tonight is that Sven is quite capable of running this farm, and take away a few hungry bellies, this place will prosper again, too. You need not answer me now. I will be in Norway perhaps a month, before I must set sail for Greenland. The seas can get unfriendly if one waits too long into the fall before making the crossing. Talk it over with your families and please let me have an answer before I return to Greenland." Thorkell's stern expression turned more optimistic.

"Now, where is some more of that mead, and get that Gerna back in here to put a smile on an old man's face," the older gentleman chuckled.

———

AFTER ERIK PRESENTED the idea to his family later that night, Tor asked, "What about the Skræling, Father? Have they become friendly?"

"I happen to believe that they were never unfriendly, son. I believe that through misunderstandings because of our language differences and our 'Norse brute mentality,' we blamed them and started all the troubles with the Skræling ourselves. My dealings with the boy, Peluk, taught me that they are a deeply spiritual people who are compassionate to all. They live in a difficult place, struggling daily to provide food and shelter for their families where the climate and dangerous animals pose a constant threat.

"Then we arrive on the scene and start taking their things without asking or offering anything in the way of a fair exchange. No wonder they respond with arrows. And, by the way, Peluk and his people did not even have bows and arrows, or horses, or many of the things we take for granted. I believe it is unfair to say that they are the problem with western expansion. If we move there, I hope to make a difference in the way we conduct business with them," Erik explained, looking frequently with challenging eyes toward Olaf.

"You may be right, and probably are, Erik. But something tells me you will not alter the way Norsemen look at the world. Most of us believe we are superior to heathens who fight wars with stone weapons. I suspect the Skræling we have met so far are a small sample of what lies across the sea. Perhaps one day, Norsemen will explore all the western lands, conquering as we go," Olaf countered.

"I suspect God will frown on us if we do," Erik said glumly.

"Well, I hope Thorkell has a successful trading visit in Bergen," Olaf said cheerfully to change the subject.

"Yes, it seems Greenland goods are in demand right now. It may well be the best time to take advantage of that," Erik sounded a bit more positive talking about the move.

"You can all move to Greenland if you like, I... we are staying here and running this farm," Sven stated emphatically, waving toward his bride to include her. "This is the only home I have known, and it has been good to me. I can still sell livestock and lumber enough to support a big estate. Actually, it would probably be better for us to split up and have holdings in both places. It appears Greenland will become a powerful colony. In the long run, it will make Norway stronger. Future prosperity will benefit us all. With our name solid in Greenland and Norway, we will become an important entity in the future of our country."

"You are showing great wisdom, little brother. Your words sound true and strong. You almost sound like someone looking to become Jarl," Erik praised Sven, then winked. "Now what do the womenfolk have to say?" He looked particularly at Erna.

Her arms were wrapped around her three-year-old daughter sitting in her lap. Both were listening intently to the men discuss their future. She hesitated, then said stoically, "Since when does it matter what women have to say about what men decide? You know you will do what you think is right, no matter what I say. The woman's place is to support her husband and make life as good as possible for her family, no matter what foolish thing he gets her into. A woman only wants a stable home, to care for her family in a place she feels comfortable. She wants a husband who works hard to provide food and shelter, keep her safe from wars and other man-made catastrophes. I feel I have that here. I am raising my children here. At the same time, I know that our economy has been better here. I hear the siren call of prosperity and hope in a new place. A place where war is far away. I know of other families who have already gone there and are supposedly doing quite well. Perhaps with Sven staying and keeping this farm, we have a place to return if things do not go well in Greenland." She looked hopefully at Sven.

"Surely you know you are always welcome here, sister-in-law. Our family will never outgrow this hall," Sven replied as he waved around the spacious room with one hand and patted his wife's belly with the other.

"Are we moving?" Gerna asked in her child's voice. "Can we take our room? I would miss the big bed. And what about my pony? Can Hrim come?" Tears started to fill her eyes.

"We are just discussing it," Erik said in his best 'father' voice.

"Are there people to make friends with there?" Tor cut into the conversation. "Is there anyone Gerna's age? Do they have game competitions so I can improve my skills? Or will it just be all work?" He asked questions as they popped into his head.

"Thorkell tells us that the Greenland settlements are growing. They hold a Thing in Brattahlid every summer now and conduct a midsummer celebration at that time. Norse from all lands are migrating there all the time, and bringing English, Irish, and Frankish thralls with them. Many of the thralls have become freemen already. It appears that politics are not nearly as complex as in Norway. I am beginning to feel the move would be a great opportunity for our family," Erik enthusiastically looked around the table as he spoke.

"If all Uncle Thorkell says is true, we would not be making a mistake in settling over there," Olaf chimed in. "We have just lost many good men fighting in England. Norway's holdings are solid there right now, and our new king seems confident. But, we have been through many kings of late, and who can tell how stable England is. As Erna says, at least Greenland is far from any war. Taking all factors into account, I think we should go."

"I will support my husband in this decision," Skjoldis said quietly. She held a young daughter on her lap as well. *Will there be suitable young men to marry her to when the time comes? Will there be any young men left in Norway, for all the warring?* Skjoldis could not keep herself from wondering.

TEN EVENINGS later and just before dark, Thorkell's horn echoed through the hills above Ulfrstadt from the fjord. *Back already?* Erik wondered. He rushed to the dock and was there, alongside Tor and Olaf, to meet Thorkell as he climbed from his knorr. "Greetings, uncle. You are back earlier than expected."

A broad smile adorned Thorkell's bearded face. "The trading has been good, boys! Bergen loves Greenland! Have you any mead left? I am in a mood for some, and I brought some Frankish wine for your wives. Heh, heh, heh!" He chuckled.

Olaf said, "My wife will prefer the mead! We will be up soon." And left for his hall after hugging Thorkell.

———

WHEN OLAF, with his wife and daughter, arrived and sat at the main table in Erik's Hall, Thorkell held up a cup of mead in a toast. "To Greenland's newest settlers!" They all raised cups of mead, wine, or milk.

"When do you think is the best time to sail, Uncle?" Olaf asked.

"The summer months bring the easiest crossings." Thorkell started. "It is a bit of a dance. If you start too early, you run into many icebergs drifting south from the Greenland Sea. Wait too long, and you can be slowed terribly by calm periods. I think mid-May is the best time. If you get ashore by June, we can have at least one main hall built by winter. You don't want to be living in tents in winter. Ha! Of course, you will stay in my hall until your farms are ready for occupation!" He beamed as he looked at the little girls and winked. "I can help provide you with livestock and barley seed, but bring what you can—new stock always helps the vigor of the herd."

"I have to build a knorr. It will take me until mid-May to be ready. And...we need to re-caulk and refit *The Sea Mare* before setting out. We will be busy between now and then," Erik added.

"Sounds like we'll be plenty busy when we get there too!" Olaf chimed in. "When are you heading back, uncle?"

"I should have my ship loaded and ready in three days. I will set to work getting lumber, nails, and other things ready for your arrival. We use a lot of sod blocks building our halls, but we won't want to cut them until construction starts. I cannot tell you all how happy it makes an old man feel to know what family he has left is willing to uproot to come and fulfill his dreams," Thorkell managed, emotionally.

"To Greenland!" Skjoldis raised her cup.

"To Greenland!" they all chimed in, Erna adding "...and family!"

Olaf would leave his mother to her hall. She would have his sister, Thordis, and her husband, Garik, to help run her affairs. Over the years, Haakon and Olaf had accumulated great hordes of silver and gold. Lokhilla was a rich woman and had many suitors now that her mourning period had ended. Olaf knew she was wise enough to select the right one. Whenever he returned, he would find a new man in charge of Haakon's Hall and wealth. That only gave him another reason to move far away.

CHAPTER 19
THE SEA OX

Once again Erik, Tor, Olaf, and Erik's master ship builder, Hjalmar took to the forests to select trees for building Erik's new knorr. It would need to hold fifty settlers and their personal belongings, along with two horses, Gerna's pony, two cows, a bull, eight sheep, four goats, and two crates of chickens. In addition, barrels of fresh water, nuts, salted meats and fish, tools, seeds for gardens and barley fields. The cargo would weigh this ship (and Olaf's) like none Erik had ever built before.

When the proper oaks, pines, spruces and birches were selected, Hjalmar took crews to harvest the trees needed to get started building the big knorr to be christened *The Sea Ox*.

The process was similar to the longships they

had built two years earlier. And Tor would join in on the building crew, doing what his eleven-year-old frame would allow. Erik explained the whole thing to him before they started work. "This will be an ocean-going knorr. It will need to be built shorter in length, but wider in the beam, deeper in the draft, and much heavier. The keel will be thicker and heavier. The ribs will have to accommodate a hold strong enough to house the livestock. That will be located just forward of the mast. And forward of that will be a hold for bedding and fodder to feed the animals on the voyage. The livestock hold will need to be cleaned twice a day to keep the animals from getting sick and keeping the air breathable for the settlers who will be sleeping on the second deck. I suspect they will be seasick as it is.

"Right behind the mast will be another hold for storing all the things we are bringing. The livestock hold will be open from the deck to the bottom of the hold so the livestock can get plenty of air. We will have a tent over the deck for shade and shelter. Behind the mast, there will be three decks. The first one will be the floor of the cargo hold. That will not be very high. Above that will be a deck for sleeping pallets. The third deck will be for the seamen to work. Like the longships, we will have rowers, but only sixteen per side. And of course, the steerboard and tiller will be in the right, rear of the ship. There will be three strakes above the oar ports. The bottom will be flatter and wider, and the ends will rise above the deck but not as much as in the longships."

"Will there be a rack for shields on the gunwales?" Tor asked.

"Yes. This is not a warship, but when we go to sea, we must be prepared for anything that might happen," Erik replied cautiously.

"I thought there were no wars in Greenland," Tor pressed the point.

"The men that we hire to man the ship are warriors, and they take their war tools with them wherever they go. So yes, they will have their swords with them, as will I...and you will have your grandfather's sword that was given when you were born. You still won't be able to wield it, but you will have it." Erik smiled at the memory of the last time Tor tried to lift that long sword.

"Maybe by the time we finish this ship, I will be strong enough," Tor said, mostly to himself.

"There will not be a dragon's head made to put on this ship," Erik said.

"I know, that is only for coastal raiders and big warships. You already explained how that works when we were building the longships. I thought that Helgi's carving was scary though," Tor said.

"Perhaps we can have him carve something special for this ship for your mother," Erik replied.

"Better not be a dragon—they scare her," Tor replied quickly.

"Did she tell you that?" Erik asked. *She never said anything about dragons scaring her to me.*

"Oh yes, many times," Tor replied matter-of-factly.

Women. "Hmf," Erik huffed.

WORKING on the days they could throughout the winter, by the end of February, the ship was taking shape. The four fingers thick oak floorboards for the livestock hold had been soaked in boiled pine pitch and were ready to nail down. Freki bored holes in the floorboards and smiled as Tor swung the heavy hammer driving nails into the joist beams below. He was impressed at how hard Tor was working on the ship and the strength he was gaining by doing so. *Tor will be a mighty man one day,* he thought. "Don't drive those nails through the bottom of the ship there, boy. I don't think ye know how strong yer gettin'! Ha-ha!"

Tor smiled and hit the nail harder.

By spring equinox, the ship was still not ready to be slid into the water. A snowy early March had caused delays in getting the needed trees out of the forest to finish the decking and several of the fittings. Erik was getting nervous.

Many of the crew would be settling in Greenland. Some of them had never been on a ship before, and he wanted the ship completed so they could take it out on the sea and get used to it some before he needed them to sail it across the ocean.

Others were seasoned sailors who wanted to return after the voyage. Erik had arranged with Einar Hagalsson to man the steerboard at night and when Erik needed to be doing something else. Einar was a veteran steersman and had been to Greenland eight times. Einar would remain under Erik's employ and would sail the ship to and from Norway selling Erik and Olaf's Greenlandic merchandise. Einar had helped Erik fill out the crew for the upcoming voyage. As their agreement went, every day after June first, Erik would have to pay these men for doing nothing.

Finally, on the first day of May, the ship was ready to be slid from the building location, over the beach to the water. Unlike the light-weight longships, *The Sea Ox* was too heavy to pick up and carry on land. The ship had been built on blocks facing the sea so that, once readied, it could be slid straight across the beach into the water. A series of short log sections of a similar diameter were lined up a couple of ells apart and while several men on each side kept it from tipping over while others pulled on ropes from the front and still others pushed from the rear. The ship was eased into the water, and when it floated, they gave a great cheer. Most of the next day was spent setting the mast, rigging the sail, and other last-minute details.

Finally, on the twelfth day of May, in the Year of Our Lord 1019, two big knorrs loaded with sailors, settlers, and the hopes and dreams of a prosperous new beginning, cast off from the docks of Ulfrstadt, Norway for the Western Settlement of Greenland. They would stop in Iceland to pick up two brothers of one member of Olaf's crew. That would also give the women and farmers aboard the ships a chance to put their feet on solid ground for a couple of days before the rest of their journey.

CHAPTER 20
THE VOYAGE

The crews strained at their oars to push the two big knorrs out into the fjord before the sun broke over the shoulder of the mountains east of Ulfrstadt. The outgoing tide helped propel the heavy ships until the sail arms could be hoisted and the sails unfurled. Just a few wispy high clouds broke the deep blue of the morning sky. It contrasted starkly with the bright greens of the forests and meadows and the dark grays of the bare rocks of the hills lining both sides of the fjord. Snow still dominated the eastern mountains, and even some of the high gullies on the north-facing slopes along the fjord. The water reflected the deep blue of the sky. From high on the hills came a cool down draft that snapped the sails full, propelling the ships toward the mouth of the fjord and the open sea.

"Notice that we stay back and to the north side of the fjord while Olaf stays a bit to the south side. That is so, as our sail catches the wind, it does not block it from his sail. That way we don't run up on him, and we stay clear of each other. Once we are in the open ocean we will be farther apart, and it will not be an issue." Erik stood at the steerboard, and Tor was glued to his side trying to learn all about sailing the ship. "Going toward the sea down the fjord we have a land breeze. That is to say that the cooler air on the mountains flows down to the warmer water and pushes the ship right to the ocean. Once we get on the open sea, the wind will determine the angle we need to set the sail. For now it is placed square with the ship."

In a hand of time, the open ocean was in full view. The seasoned crew members welcomed the sight, while those their first time on open seas wondered what they had gotten themselves into. In the far distance, the horizon became a blurry mist, converging the sea with the sky at some undetectable location. As they entered the sea, the swells were barely noticeably bigger than the small waves in the fjord. Both ships rocked gently as they sailed due west.

"This keeps up, we'll be eatin' fresh salmon in

Iceland day after tomorrow!" a first-time crew member yelled back to Erik at the steerboard.

"Beautiful day for sure," Erik replied. *Now don't go putting a hex on us, Gimli.* The seasoned men around Gimli quickly reprimanded him about predicting the future while under sail. After two more hands of time, Erik pointed to the south to show Tor the very tops of the hills of the Shetland Islands. Tor stood next to Erik and looked on in wonder.

"They look so small!" Tor exclaimed. "How can people and sheep live on such a small land?" he asked.

"The hills look small because they are so far away. If you sailed up to them, you would marvel at how big they are. Have you looked behind us of late? Look how small the homeland is becoming." Erik smiled.

"When will it disappear, Father?" Tor asked.

"By morning you will only be able to tell there are mountains there by the clouds above the highest peaks," Erik said. "And when we look north, we will see the Faroes. The horizon will put the sea at halfway up the mountains at noon, if we are on our proper course."

"Tell me again how we know where we are when we can see so little land," Tor requested.

"Here, take the steerboard while I explain it

again. It will be easier to understand now that we are out here."

"What if I don't steer right?"

"I am right here, just stay behind Olaf. He knows where we are," Erik explained as he switched positions with Tor. Then he reached into his bag that lay next to the side of the ship. Tor recognized the sun compass that Erik brought out. "As it turns out, Ulfrfjord lays just about due east of the southern tip of Greenland. If we sail due west from here, we will arrive just where we want to. From there we follow the coast to the Western Settlements.

"You see this line right here?" He pointed to one of the lines that radiated in a curve from one of the points on the dial face. "We know that in about two hands of time, or two hours, the sun will be at its highest place in the sky, noon. So, if I hold this disk flat, the sun makes a shadow from this pin in the middle of the dial. Now see how the tip of the pin's shadow comes close to this line on the dial? That tells me that the ship is on the same line I want it to be on. When the sun is at its peak, the pointer's shadow will be right at the line on the dial. If the shadow lies above this line, then we are too far north, if it does not reach this line, we are too far south. This way we can stay at the right latitude as we sail across the ocean. Notice those lines radiate from each of the eight principal directions. We are on the west line for this voyage. And when we come back from Greenland selling our merchandise, we will use the east line. When we see the sea birds south of Iceland, we will turn northwest until we see the coastline, then we will follow it to the port of Borg on the Borgarnes fjord on the southwest side of the island."

"How do we do this at night?" Tor asked.

"Einar will have the steerboard after the sun sets, and he knows how to steer by the stars, as does Bjarni on Olaf's ship. By knowing the hour and the location of the north or pole star, a good seaman can know right where he is and where he needs to go. So, you see, we are never lost," Erik explained confidently.

"What about when it is cloudy or storming?" Tor asked.

"We just need to stay in sight of Olaf. He has a sunstone. A piece of a special rock that tells him the location of the sun. It works day or night in any weather."

"Do you have one?"

"No, I have never had the chance to learn how to use one. They are very rare and complicated to use. Olaf might show it to you someday. It is very precious. Olaf got his from Haakon, and he guards it closely," Erik answered.

As the sun was setting, the sky remained cloudless for the most part and a steady southeast breeze propelled them at a good pace through low swells. Erik thanked God for a smooth start to their voyage.

"You must be tired, you have been at that steerbord all day," Einar said as he walked up, still looking through sleepy eyes.

"Yes, I could use some rest. Tor here has been keeping us on course pretty well. We have only had to trim the sail a couple of times. It has stayed full all day under a steady breeze. It has just started to slacken a little, but still enough to keep the sail full. Olaf has held a steady course," Erik reported to Einar. "He will burn that lamp, as we will ours, so that we can see each other at all times."

"Get some sleep, and I will see you at sunrise. Tor you rest those arms for tomorrow," Einar replied cheerfully.

By morning there were only a few high clouds to be seen far to the west. The sun came up orange and yellow without a hint of clouds behind them. The breeze was still steady out of the southeast, and the swells were still low. There was not a hint of land in sight as Erik emerged from the big tent running down the center of the ship.

Tor was in the animal hold cleaning the previous night's bedding from the animal pens.

New straw bedding was laid down in all the stalls. The animals had calmed down from their frightful walk down the steep ramp into the ship. Not even the goats had wanted any part of it. But now they were resigned to their new fate of standing at the bottom of a ship as it rode up and down rhythmically over the sea. Sleep came easy for them. Tor put the old bedding in a large wool sack, then fed the horses some oats and fresh hay, the cattle and sheep got fresh hay as well. When Gerna got up and around, he would bring her down here so she could give her pony a carrot. The goats were given table scraps from last night's meal and the morning's breakfast. While they were eating, Tor and a peasant boy milked the two nannies and the two milk cows. Tor then hauled the sack of old animal bedding up to the main deck where it was dumped overboard. At home it would be stored and put on fields and garden plots.

The sun was well up when Tor finally joined Erik at the steerboard. "You can barely see the tops of the Faroes if you look northwest along the horizon," Erik pointed the tiny dark bumps out to Tor. "By midday the tops of those mountains will be half above the horizon and straight north of us."

"I have never known the world was this round," Tor observed. "You can see the curve on the horizon and how the lands grow or shrink as we get closer or farther away."

The day passed eventless. The breeze swung to more south as the day progressed, some minor sail trimming was needed. The sun stayed bright all day.

———

BY THE NEXT MORNING, more clouds were present in the southwest, and the sun came up through a veil of broken low clouds making the eastern sky appear as if it were a curtain of fire.

"You won't see a sunrise prettier than today," Einar yawned as Erik came to relieve him.

"Agreed! God in his glory!" Erik exclaimed.

Einar nodded. "Wake me when we get close to the coast."

"I shall," Erik said cheerfully. *Looks like another fine day!* The northern horizon just faded from sky to sea. But Erik noted that the breeze was increasing out of the south. He had not seen the sail this strained against the lines yet this voyage, and the swells were twice what they had been. The ship was gradually rolling much more as it slid through the seas. Tor had to steady himself as he came back to join Erik.

"How is your sister this morning?" Erik asked.

"I don't know, she was not awake when I finished the chores and came out here," Tor replied. For the third day, the air was warm enough for just his blue long-sleeve tunic and wool pants held up by shoulder straps. He wore a pointed knit wool hat with floppy ear muffs covering his head. Straight straw yellow hair hung down his neck, teased by the wind. His face did not yet grow more than invisible fuzz. His blue eyes shone bright in the early morning sun.

"Look, Tor!" Erik pointed to a whale spout off the starboard side of the ship. "We are closing in on the Iceland waters." He looked up at the sun and said, "Right about on time."

Olaf was already easing his ship around to a northwest course. "I better take the steerboard now." Erik eased in to take Tor's place.

Tor stepped back and watched his father take over.

"We will be riding the wind as we turn, men, be ready to square the sail!" he yelled.

Tor clung to the gunwale as the ship swung. It seemed to slow down briefly until the sail snapped full once again, and they accelerated. Now they were running with the growing swells, and their speed increased. The up-and-down movement increased as the waves grew. Suddenly seagulls were in the sky. Tor looked north as the white skyline of Iceland's mountains broke the horizon. A thin line of black mist rose from an area west of the center. It looked like smoke.

"We should make port by midafternoon!" Erik exclaimed above the growing wind.

"What is that smoke from, Father? Is someone's hall on fire?" Tor asked in a worried tone.

"No. That is a volcano. Iceland is the land of fire and ice. Often the land belches fire and smoke there. No one lives near that area so there is no danger," Erik answered nonchalantly.

CHAPTER 21
STORM

Tor looked closer at the northern horizon, and something seemed wrong. Behind the mountains the sky looked dark, almost black. *Is the sea belching fire and smoke to the north?* he wondered.

As they proceeded north by northwest, the men started to notice the menacing sky. A big storm was moving south, and as it did, it sucked the air into it. The wind at their back was increasing. Ahead, the black wall began to envelop the growing landform of Iceland. Lightning could be seen among the billowing tops of those clouds.

By the time Erik could see the entire coastline, the ship was riding up and over waves higher than the prow post. The sky ahead turned black and threatening. Lightning bolts were flashing among and from the clouds constantly. A continuous rumble of thunder rolled from the storm. Water spouts could be seen dancing across the waves far in front of them. They were going to lose the race to get into the protection of the fjord before the storm hit them. He glanced at Olaf's ship as it rode up a wave. His men were frantically lowering the sail arm. He gave the order to do the same.

"Tor, get in the tent and tie everything and everyone down, including you!" Erik yelled above the wind and thunder. Tor crawled to the tent flap.

In the tent, everyone was becoming seasick. Buckets of vomit were sliding across the deck as the ship tossed in the seas. The animals were in full panic, neighing, bellowing, stomping and trying to escape their confinement.

Gerna still lay in her bedding, Erna washing her face with a wet rag. "Mother, what is wrong?" Tor yelled out.

"I don't know, she has had a fever all morning, but now it has gotten far worse. I wish Lokhilla were here!" His mother sounded worried.

"Shall I go get Father?" was all he could think to say.

"No, his hands are full guiding the ship!" she yelled back.

"He said to tie everything and everyone down! I will tend to that!" Tor yelled as he made his way around the other settlers urging them to tie themselves to anything solid on the ship.

Erik panicked as he watched the wall of water advancing toward them. It was higher than the mast and marked the point where the waves changed course from rolling from the south to north in an instant. He had never witnessed such an abrupt change. He prayed the ship would hold together. Erik ordered oars into the water to help him keep the ship pointed into that monster wave. He watched in terror as Olaf's ship rode up the big wave. Olaf's ship broke over the top, water spraying everywhere, and disappeared down the back of the huge wave. His own ship rode to the bottom of the trough. His eyes bulged at the enormous wave bearing down on them. A second later they were thrown up as the wave advanced. To his surprise, *The Sea Ox* rode to the top of the wave, stalled a heartbeat and plunged down the back side. Suddenly they were in a deluge of icy rain.

Only Einar, who had woken up when the waves started getting wild, came on deck with anything resembling cold weather gear. He had been through enough storms to know what was needed.

"Give me the steerboard while you go get some warm rain gear on!" he yelled to Erik.

"Good idea! This rain is cold as mid-winter! I

will tell the men to go, one at a time to do the same!" Erik yelled as the ship started riding up the next wave. A flash of lightning showed *The Sea Mare* being pushed south on the same wave. Nothing could stand up to the gale blowing out of the north. Rain was pelting them like a volley of arrows against a shield-wall.

As Erik ducked into the tent structure, he was astonished at the chaos. Vomit spread across the floor from spilled buckets. Blankets, ropes, chairs, and people were among the things wadded in knots everywhere. From the animal hold there came a terrifying cacophony of sounds from the animals. In a panic, Erik finally found his family. Erna had been seasick and was weak from the retching. Gerna was in her arms, burning up with fever and vomit clinging to her mouth. Tor was up against the side tied to rib with vomit spewed down the front of him and looking pathetic.

"What can I do for you, woman?" he cried out hopelessly as the ship once again was riding up the face of a wave. Somehow Einar had managed to make a turn while the ship was in the trough so now they were riding with the waves, if that would make a difference. *How long will this storm last?* he wondered. "Tor, you must get up and move! Get some men and boys and start bailing water from the bilge! It will help with your seasickness!"

Water from the rain and splashing from the waves was flowing under the skirt of the tent. The walls were flapping furiously in the wind. Rain was starting to be driven through the boiled linseed oil soaked wool fabric.

"Get us ashore so I can tend to this sick girl!" Erna lashed out.

"I will see what can be done!" he answered and started making his way back.

Erik struggled to make his way to the rear of the ship. The storm had intensified, winds blowing the rain horizontally from rear to front, rain was coming down in buckets, lightning lashed and slashed across the sky with terrifying frequency. Though it was no later than midafternoon, the sky would be pitch black were it not for the lightning. Every now and then Erik caught a glimpse of Olaf's ship farther to what Erik thought was the west. From what he could see, Olaf's tent was in tatters, flapping in the wind. *How long can ours last?* The huge waves were pushing them at a furious pace, either south or west. He could no longer be certain.

Erik worked his way around the ship checking on everyone. He did not even try to talk above the howling wind and the continuous thunder. He just patted the sailors on the back and made sure they were tied to their chests. Several were shivering against the icy rain. *This storm must have formed over Greenland. It cannot go on much longer without blowing itself out, can it?*

Day passing into night and night passing into day went without notice. The storm was so intense, daylight did nothing to brighten the sky. Somehow the ship stayed together and floated. Crews took shifts baling water from the hold which had become a continuous job. One horse broke a leg scrambling in its tight stall, trying to escape. The other one fell during the violent rocking, slamming into the railing between stalls, and landed on the injured horse. In the thrashing that ensued, the injured horse suffocated, and the other drove the splintered rail into its side causing a slow, painful death. No humans knew anything had happened until it was too late to save either animal.

A small boy slipped from his mother's grip and dashed his head against the deck and died. Misery abounded aboard *The Sea Ox*.

At some point in time, Erik had lost all sight of *The Sea Mare*. He did not know if it just drifted out of sight or went down. Every minute seemed like eternity as lightning still flashed with frightening frequency and intensity. The cold wind continued to howl. Erik and Einar struggled to keep the ship riding with the waves. More times than Erik could count, water crashed over the gunwales. The baling crews worked nonstop to keep water from accumulating too deep in the hold.

On one of his trips around the deck checking on the oarsmen, Erik found an oar flopping around. The oarsman slumped awkwardly across his sea chest. The man was dead. Hypothermia, Erik guessed. Two others were close to it. *Must get these men inside the shelter.* He went to Einar and told him what happened. They decided to get the men into the tent. The oars were not helping that much anyway. They shipped oars and closed the oar ports. By the time all were accounted for, three men were dead.

In the tent, things were no better. Everyone was freezing. Erna sat propped against a chest tied to the floor holding Gerna. But the little girl had died. Erna was in shock and just flopped about as the ship jerked back and forth and up and down in the storm-tossed sea. Erik tried to stir Erna, but she would have none of it. She refused to do anything but sit there rocking the eight-year-old child's corpse. He held his wife's hand trying desperately to coax her into action.

Suddenly a tremendous cracking sound, followed by a deafening clap of thunder. Smoke oozed from the grain of the mast. Then a series of loud popping noises. Erik looked on in horror as a bulge appeared in the mast just below the upper deck boards. He opened his chest, grabbed his axe, and scrambled outside.

In the light from lightning bolts, he could see the mast was broken. The tight stay lines were holding it up momentarily, but he knew that would not last. The lines needed to be cut and the mast freed from the rigging and cast overboard as quickly as possible. Just then the heavy mast canted sideways and came down with a crash, destroying the fore ridgepole of the tent. Women screamed, and men started shouting. Erik looked and saw that a two-ell section of the forward starboard gunwale was broken. He went to the aft tie blocks and hacked the rigging holding the mast free. Gimli had emerged up front and did the same up there. Other men appeared and together they wrestled the mast off the ship.

TOTAL DARKNESS SHROUDED the mid deck of *The Sea Ox*. With the storm raging, it was impossible for Tor to see a thing. The constant jostling, lurching, bobbing, and jerking made hanging on to something solid the highest priority. Moaning and crying told him where clusters of the ship's passengers huddled. Unseen, the bulging grain of the pine pole that was the ship's mast exploded when the above deck section finally toppled. The loud cracking noise was drowned out by thunderous roar of thunder, wind, human, and animal screams.

A splinter as long and as big around as a man's arm flew across the area between the upper and lower decks. Erna did not even look up as the huge projectile flew at her. It slammed into the side of her head like a war club. She never knew what hit her. Tor, his head pressed against Erna's leg, felt her stiffen momentarily, twitch, then go limp. When he dared to reach up from his prone position, flattened on the mid deck next to her, he felt her neck stretched at an odd angle. When he found her face and the side of her head, he could feel her warm blood and misshapen head. He knew instantly that she was dead, Gerna's body still cradled in her lifeless arms. Tor scrambled to find his way to the upper deck.

"Father, Father! Where are you? Father, where are you? It's Mother...Father, where are you?" he shouted into the night, voice nearly drowned by the rolling thunder and gale-force winds.

"Easy boy," Einar shouted. "Listen to me!"

"What do you want? Where is Father?" Tor demanded.

"That is what I am trying to tell you, boy. Your father is not here. The mast caught on him and yanked him overboard. I could not find him. The water is too cold. He is gone by now." Einar's voice was filled with sadness.

"No, it is not possible! First Gerna died of a fever, then a large splinter from the mast killed Mother. Now you tell me Father is dead. No! This cannot be happening. We are all going to die!" he screamed, tears flowing from his eyes.

As THE JAGGED butt of the mast slid and rolled off the gunwale into the frothing sea, a large splinter caught in Erik's heavy wool overcoat sleeve and yanked him overboard. The weight and inertia of the mast tore through the thick sleeve and gouged deeply into Erik's upper left arm and ripped the fabric away. Frantically, Einar searched for the ship's master, hoping a line could reach him. Alas, there was no coming back from that sea.

The cold water hit Erik like a boulder falling on him. It took his breath away in less than a heartbeat. He fought his way to the surface and saw nothing but black as he desperately gulped air. Lightning flashed, and he saw the aft end of the ship thirty ells away. Somehow, his left arm would not respond to his command, causing him great difficulty in moving it. Lightning flashed again, and he saw he was swimming in bloody water. He reached over and felt his left arm with his right hand. He thought he could feel his upper arm bone, but his fingers were so numb he could not be sure. Much of the flesh and muscle had been ripped away. Lightning flashed again; the ship was twice as far away. The cold water was numbing his senses and stealing his strength. His heavy woolen clothes, drenched in freezing water, was too much for him to overcome. Erik felt his body losing the battle against the turbulent, frigid sea. *Erna and Tor, I pray you can forgive me*. The icy water engulfed him for the last time as Erik Haraldsson sank to his watery grave.

The crippled knorr continued to ride the storm-driven waves while being pushed south and west. Tor was now an orphan and the owner of a disabled ship being pushed to who knew where?

A LOOK AT BOOK TWO
TOR'S SAGA

In a tale of survival and discovery, one Norse warrior's quest for belonging begins.

Tor Haraldsson is far from his homeland. The lone survivor of a shipwreck, he has been washed ashore on an unfamiliar beach and rescued by a compassionate Lenni Lenape family. Adopted into their clan, he grows into a formidable warrior, catching the attention of a powerful Cahokia chief.

Learning to communicate with the people who have taken him in and still remaining cut off from any Norse settlements, Tor faces the daunting challenge of surviving and thriving in an unfamiliar land. With no knowledge of his location, he must forge a path in a world unlike any he has ever known to get back to his only living family in Greenland.

Amid vivid portrayals of an ancient, complicated land, Tor must find a way to reconnect with his roots—or carve out a new destiny in a world of fresh alliances and old conflicts.

Embark on an epic journey as a fierce warrior navigates an untamed world, finding his place in it and within himself.

AVAILABLE OCTOBER 2024

ABOUT THE AUTHOR

Ron Briggs is a veteran, having served four years in the USAF. His education includes a Bachelor of Science in Range and Wildlife Ecology at Oklahoma State University and a Master of Science in Range and Wildlife Management at Texas A&I University.

He is retired from the USDA-Natural Resources Conservation Service, and his career encompassed twenty-five years as District Conservationist in Linn County, Kansas. Prior to college, he worked seven years in the building trades.

Having developed a deep interest in history, especially in the pre-colonial period of North America, Ron's interests prompted him to begin researching a pre-history story about the Tallgrass Prairie Region of the Great Plains. That research evolved into his current multi-volume work, the Yellow Hair series, which includes scenes from northern Europe to the mountains of western North America.

Ron and his wife, Debbie, currently live in Mound City, Kansas, and have two grown children and seven grandchildren. His interests include spending time with family, writing, hunting, fishing, traveling, and woodworking.

BIBLIOGRAPHY

Appelt, Martin."Man, Culture and Environment in Ancient Greenland," *Publication No. 4*, Danish Polar Center.

Bierhorst, John.*Mythology of the Lanape: Guide and Texts.*University of Arizona Press, 1995.

Bronsted, Johannes. *The Vikings.* London: Penguin Books, 1960, Revised 1965.

Clarke, Helen and Bjorn Ambrosiani. *Towns in the Viking Age.* New York: St. Martin's Press, 1991.

Cohat, Yves and Ruth Daniel, tr. *The Vikings: Lords of the Seas.* Gallimard, 1987.

Damas, David. *Arctic, Vol. 5, Handbook of North American Indians.* Washington, D.C.: Smithsonian Press, 1984.

Charles River, ed. *Native American Tribes: The History and Culture of the Inuit (Eskimos).*

Feasel, Charles T. *White Bear.* New York: Ballantine Books, 1990.

Fitzhugh, William and Elizabeth Ward. *Vikings, The North Atlantic Saga.* Washington, D.C.: Smithsonian Press, 2000..

Gordon, E. V., rev by A. R. Taylor. *An Introduction to Old Norse.* London:Oxford Press.

Gronnow, Bjarni. *Late Dorset in High Arctic Greenland: Final Report on the Gateway to Greenland Project.* Canadian Archeological Association, 1999.

Grumet, Robert S. *The Lenapes (Indians of North America).* Chelsea House Publishing, 1989.

Harrington, Mark R. *Religion and Ceremonies of the Lenape.* Forgotten Books, 2012.

Harrington, Mark R. . *The Indians of New Jersey, Dickon Among the Lanapes.* New Jersey: Rutgers University Press, 1966

Heckewelder, John Gotlieb Ernestus, notes by William C. Reichel. *History, Manners, and Customs of The Indian Nations*

Who Inhabited Pennsylvania and the Neighbouring States. Historical Society of Pennsylvania, 1881

Ingstad, Anne Stine et al. *The Discovery oy a Norse Settlement in America. Excavations at L'Anse aux Meadows, Newfoundland, 1961-1968.* Tromso, 1977.

Jones, Gwynne. *A History of the Vikings.* Oxford University Press, 1968, 1973, 1984.

Kunz, Keneva, tr. and Gisli Sigurdsson, ed.The Vinland Sags. London: Penguin Books, 2008.

McCullough, K. M. "The Ruin Islanders: Thule Culture Pioneers in the High Eastern Arctic," Archeological Survey of Canada 141, Canadian Museum of Civilization, 1989.

McGee, Robert. *Ancient People of the Arctic.* Vancouver: University of British Columbia Press, 1996.

McGee, Robert. *The Last Imaginary Place.* New York: Oxford University Press, 2005.

Mcleod, William Christi. "The Family Hunting Territory and Lenape Political Organization," American Anthropology 24.

Maschner, Herbert, Masson, Owen, McGee, Robert *The Northern World AD 900-1400.* Salt Lake City: The University of Utah Press, 2009.

Maxwell, Moreau S. *Prehistory of the Eastern Arctic.* New York: Academic Press, 1985.

Means, Bernard K. *Circular Villages of the Monongahela Tradition.* Tuskaloosa: The University of Alabama Press, 2007.

Rasmusen, Knud. *Eskimo Folk Tales.* Copenhagen: Gyldendal, 1921.

Roesdahl, Else. *The Vikings.* New York: Penguin Books, 1987.

Schledermann, Peter. *Crossroads to Greenland, 3000 Years of Prehistory in the Eastern High Arctic.* The Arctic Institute of North America of the University of Calgary, 1990.

Seaver, Kirsten A. *The Frozen Echo, Greenland and the Exploration of North America, ca. A.D. 1000-1500.* Stanford, CA: Stanford University Press, 1996.

BIBLIOGRAPHY

Simpson, Jacqueline. *Everyday Life in the Viking Age*. New York: Dorset Press, 1967.

Sutherland, Patricia, ed. *Contributions to the Study of Dorset Paleo Eskimos*. Canada Museum of History, 2005.

Trigger, Bruce G. *Northeast, Vol 15, Handbook of North American Indians*. Washington, D.C.: Smithsonian Institution Press, 1984.

Weslager, C. A. *The Delaware Indians: A History*. New Jersey: Rutgers University Press, 1972.